HONOR THY MOTHER AND FATHER

A STORY BY LILLY BUCHANAN

THE WRIGHT HOUSE

The Wright House
1985
Lilly Buchanan

The Wright House

Lilly Buchanan

Published by Lilly Buchanan, 2024.

THE WRIGHT HOUSE

First edition. April 8, 2024.

Copyright © 2024 Lilly Buchanan.

ISBN: 979-8224468560

Written by Lilly Buchanan.

This book is dedicated to all Law Enforcement Agencies.
Thank you for all you do.God Bless and protect each of you.

Beneke, you rock!

Dedicated to my brother Darby. Thank You for always being my safe place. I love you so much!

On Saturday, August 15, 1985, at 9:15 a.m. an anonymous telephone call is made to the 911 emergency call center.

"Please send police officers to check on the people who live at 1313 Marina Coffee Place. The front door is open but no one answers when I call out. They are very old. I am very concerned. I, um, I brought a coffee cake for them."

"Ma'am? What is your name?"

The caller hangs up.

Dispatch sends for a unit to meet at 1313 Marina Coffee Place, to do a welfare check.

"Patrol, the caller is an unknown female. The call originated from a pay phone."

Five minutes later, the first officers arrive, they knock on the kitchen door, and call out, "Police, anyone home?" The kitchen door is unlocked, they open it and look in. Officer Petri sees an elderly male lying face down in a pool of blood, a large kitchen knife protruding from his back. There is a lot of blood surrounding the body. Officer Petri carefully tries to feel for a pulse but there is not one. He puts his finger to his lips, telling the other officer to be quiet, and motions for Officer Griffin to follow him to search the rest of the house.

They remove their guns from their holsters and check in case the killer is still in the house. A second victim, an elderly female is in the hallway. She is deceased and is in full rigor mortise. Officer Griffin is fairly new on patrol and he is upset to see the old lady in that condition. Her hand is up in the air trying to block the blows that came her way. The house is clear, there is no one else in the house.

Officer Griffen is more than a little shaken up. This is his first dead body. The police academy didn't prepare him for this. The woman's body looks like a mannequin, posed like that. It appears her arm is raised, however, the elderly lady's elbow is resting on her rib cage propping up her arm. Her eyes are wide with terror. The dirt and broken clay pot mean she has been hit over the head with a large flower pot. A jagged piece of the flower pot has been used to stab her in the jugular vein. She is in a pool of blood. The officers do not check her for a pulse. She has a house arrest monitor on her right ankle.

About 8 feet from her is a small poodle. The poodle has been decapitated. Its body appears to be severely abused. The officers can see its ribs under its skin.

Officer Petri calls dispatch on his radio.

"Dispatch, will you please contact homicide detectives and the coroner, and get them en route to this address? We have 2 deceased victims, one elderly male, and one elderly female. We also need Sgt Wiley to 9010 (meet) with us here please."

Sgt. Wiley is their Patrol Sergeant. He is listening and breaks into the radio conversation and instructs them to go to channel 4, to free up the main channel. "I'm en route to you right now. Secure the area."

"10-4 Sgt."

Officer Petri says to the other officer, "Griffin you secure the back door and I will take the front door until homicide gets here. Man, this is a bad scene, you okay?" He notices Griffin looks pale.

"Yeah, but I am definitely calling my grandma when I get off. This is nothing like they describe it in the Academy."

"Yeah, nothing takes the place of real life. Some days this job sucks. We just have to do what we can. I'm not saying you will get used to scenes like this, but someone has to do it, and we are it."

They both go guard the doors so no one but other officers can come into the house.

There is something morbid about death. It brings out the worst in some people...voyeurs. They will camp out in the yard, or even trees just to get a glimpse of a suspect, a body, or even a murder weapon. Blood incites some people into a frenzy. Last year they had 14 murders in their small town, which believe it or not is not a big number. Larger cities have hundreds of murders a year and even more deaths by other means. But even in their small town, the neighbors come out in droves to see something, anything, so they can talk about it, speculate, and analyze it. The police chief always has to add to his statement, "Anyone caught adding lies to the investigation will be prosecuted with filing a false report and hindering an investigation. The penalty is up to 3 years imprisonment and a $10,000 fine."

This became necessary after Police Officers and Sheriff Deputies wasted hundreds of man-hours chasing the wrong suspect due to gossip, lies, and false statements in previous cases. There was a mean, hated man, Roger Tilman, the entire town hated the guy. They wanted him to be the one who took the child so badly. They wanted him out of their neighborhood and community. He was a registered sex offender. He had been arrested numerous times in his youth for being drunk and disorderly and only once, for having sex with a minor. She was 16 years old. He claims she told him she was 18. Her parents pressed charges. He served 5 years and had to register as a sex offender. So, when a child went missing, fingers were pointed at him, lies were told, and countless hours of investigations were wasted trying to make a case against him, when in fact it was the child's stepfather who had kidnapped and killed the child.

Detective Kevin Nugent enters the residence through the kitchen door. He nods to Officer Griffen but does not speak.

It is like walking into his grandmother's kitchen in the late 1960's. Avocado green refrigerator and stove, green appliances line the counter, green and white checkered pattern linoleum floors, and the countertops are white Corian. The only difference in the kitchens is the dead guy face down on the floor with the knife sticking out of his back. His grandma's kitchen didn't have one of those.

The second detective comes through the front door, Mark Tope calls, "Nugent is that you?"

"Yes, I'm visiting the dead guy in the kitchen."

"Um, join me in the hallway, and let me introduce you to the dead woman."

Detective Nugent shakes his head and wipes his face with his hand. This job is making him and his partner crazy.

The elderly lady's eyes are open, not just open, open wide with terror. Not something they are used to seeing. Most victim's eyes are closed or just have a generic stare. This lady knew she was being killed. Her right arm was raised to try and block the final blow that pierced her jugular vein, causing her to bleed out and die. She knew her attacker.

Detective Tope hands Nugent some paper booties to put over his shoes. It is standard practice nowadays to protect the crime scene.

The crime scene photographer, Brad Plant comes in and Tope yells, "Stop! Booties!"

"Hello to you too! I'm putting them on now." Plant says with a disgusted tone. He hates wearing those stupid paper booties.

Tope grumbles under his breath. Plant is forever forgetting the booties and Tope doesn't want to lose any evidence. He has a feeling this will be a difficult case.

If Plant wasn't such an amazing photographer the homicide detectives would have begged for his transfer, but the guy is a genius. He seems to find details with his camera lens that 20 pairs of eyes miss. There are problems, Plant is incredibly arrogant. He knows he is good and the second problem is he is getting famous. Other agencies are constantly trying to steal him away. There was a big meeting with the squad Lieutenant, The Captain, The Major, and the Chief of Police. They asked him to stay 7 years and then they would recommend him to the FBI academy, he counteroffered to stay 5 years, with a fast-track promotion to Captain, then a recommendation to the FBI academy. They reluctantly agree as long as he trains his replacement. He agreed as long as he could hand-pick his replacement. He wants to train him as an assistant and move him gradually into his spot. He also requests a dark room be built next to his office; the brass agrees They have no choice. He has them by their brass balls.

As Detective Plant is taking his pictures, he calls out, "Hey guys, your victim, he is Boyd Wright. He used to have the largest Ford dealership in the entire state of Washington."

Nugent answers, "Then I wonder why is he living like this. There is barely any furniture in here. The car in the driveway is a Dodge and it is at least 5 years old."

Plant says, "He had a bad heart attack years ago. Ended up turning his business over to his son. Who successfully and quickly ran it into the ground. The son quit paying the employees, the taxes, and the insurance. They lost everything. Mr. Wright had to go bankrupt. There were huge articles in the newspaper and big news stories about it on channel 17. I think that was about 2 or 3 years ago. Since then, no word about him. I kinda thought he was already dead."

Detective Tope walks outside to speak with Sgt. Wiley. The crowd had grown large. "Hey Wiley will you call for the coroner again?"

Sgt. Wiley said, "Sure thing Mark. There was a double suicide on Fork Street, so that is probably why he is running behind."

At that moment they look up to see a black F150 coming down the road at a high rate of speed. The driver slides sideways nearly hitting several onlookers. A large man, approximately 6'6, with huge muscles, jumps out of the truck and starts running towards the house. Officer Velez tries to stop him and he slams the officer to the ground. He almost makes it to the front door when 3 patrol officers tackle him to the ground and handcuff him. He begins screaming, "I'm the son. I'm the son."

They put him in the back of the nearest patrol car. Officer McDaniel speaks to him and says, "Listen, sir, you cannot go in there. We cannot let you go inside."

The man begins to sob. "Are they okay? Can you tell them I'm here? They are my parents!"

Officer McDaniel starts to answer him, but then he realizes, that although the man is sobbing hysterically, there are no tears are coming from the man's face. He closes the patrol door.

Detective Tope asked Officer Velez to get the man's shoes for evidence, there is a partial print in

the blood near the male victim.

Officer Velez opens the back of the patrol car and tells the man," I'm going to need your shoes,

sir."

The big man starts to curse and kick Officer Velez. He is berating him for being Hispanic. He kicks at the officer, and screams, "You stinking wet back. Don't you dare touch me. Go back to your own country boy."

Officer Velez is able to remove the shoes and close the door. He walks over to the other officers and says, "As you can tell he has a problem with minorities, so I need you guys to get his socks. He has blood on his left sock. It might mean something."

Officers Smith and White walk over and open the patrol door. The man is calm and allows them to remove his socks.

Officer McDaniel gets into the driver's seat of his patrol car.

"Sir I need your full name for the report please."

"Ray Wright. Hey, can I see my folks now? Don't tell them I scuffled with that spic."

"What is your address please?"

"1542 Esmond Road."

"Married?"

"Separated."

"Wife's name?"

"Satan."

"Sir, wife's name," McDonald said again, with a sigh.

"Brenda Louisa Wright."

"Her address."

"4545 Shenandoah Street.'

"Telephone number?"

"555-4545, Look can you tell me what is going on?"

"The detectives will be discussing everything with you. I do not have all of the information."

The officer gets out of the patrol car and calls dispatch with the wife's information.

Brenda Wright arrives about 10 minutes later. Sgt. Wiley meets with her. She looks briefly at Ray in the back of the patrol car. She does not look surprised. He is always doing something stupid so why should today be any different?

When Sgt. Wiley gives her the death notice, she does not react, not one tear for her in-laws. Sgt. Wiley goes inside to let the detectives know she is there and did not respond to the death notice. She did not even ask how they died. Detective Nugent comes outside and asks Brenda to meet them at their office in one hour, and she agrees.

Sgt. Wiley gets on his intercom system and starts to disperse the crowd that has gathered outside the residence.

"Anyone still here in 5 minutes will be arrested for trespassing. There is an ongoing investigation that you are hindering if you are not helping. If you have pertinent information, please give your name and telephone number to an officer... you will be contacted."

Detective Plant has already taken pictures of all the onlookers. Sometimes killers like to hang around in the crowd and watch what is happening. When officers start trying to get names and telephone numbers, the people who don't want to get involved leave quicker than the others.

The coroner and the forensic team finally arrive. After 3 hours of investigation, the homicide detectives release the victims to the coroner.

Detective Tope asks the coroner to take the Wright's little dog, (a poodle) for an examination. As I told you before, he has been decapitated.

The detectives want to keep this information out of the news. The coroner says, "Mark, it is highly unusual to examine a dog, but I will agree to the examination if it will assist with the investigation."

"It could be the key to everything, or nothing Sam. I would really appreciate it."

The coroner leaves with all 3 of the bodies, and the gawkers drift away.

Detective Plant was able to take hundreds of pictures.

Detectives Nugent and Tope go door to door to try and interview neighbors. Ironically, no one would answer their doors. There are 5 houses to the left, 5 houses to the right of the Wright's residence, and 3 directly across the street. Not one person opens the door. The detectives leave their business cards on all of the doors. Then they head back to their office to meet with Brenda Wright. She is waiting for them. Their secretary Madge has put her in a small interview room. The detectives observe her through a 2-way mirror. She is a petite, maybe 5' tall, blonde. She is drinking a Coca-Cola, is nicely dressed, and appears to be calm.

"We apologize for the wait ma'am." Detective Tope says.

Brenda shrugs her shoulders, and says, "No biggie."

"Please state your name for the record."

"Brenda Louisa Wright."

"When was the last time you saw your in-laws, Brenda?"

"Well, Agnes came to my house a month ago. Ray told her that I threw him out, so she came to beg me to take him back. When I told her no, she started chewing me out. We had some real nasty words, she stomped her foot at me, then left."

"Have you talked to her since?"

"Yes, she called yesterday (Friday) at about 10:00 in the morning, demanding that I let Glenn, my 23-year-old son, move back in with me. He's been staying with them. Apparently, it's not been going too good over there. Look, Glenn is a grown man. He is 23 years old. He is not my problem anymore. I raised him. He turned out like his daddy. I did the best I could but he is awful. He was in jail for drugs. The condition of his release was he had to live with family. Ray fixed it so that Glenn would live with his grandparents, under house arrest. He couldn't live with Ray and me because Ray has past felonies. She was insisting I take him now that Ray is out of the house, but I said no. She told me to go to hell and hung up."

"Do you think your son or your husband could hurt them?"

"No. I don't. Even though they are jerks, it's just talk."

"Do you know anyone who would want to hurt them?"

"No, no I don't."

"Do you have any theories about what could have happened?"

"I have no idea. A robbery gone bad? I just don't know."

"Did the Wrights have anything of value?"

"Well Boyd had an expensive, antique Bourbon collection and he collected signed baseball cards. Agnes had jewelry and expensive dishware." Brenda answers.

The two detectives look at each other, both aware that none of those items were in the house when they investigated the murders.

"How would you describe your relationship with your in-laws Brenda?"

"I really didn't associate with them much. I have my own life now that Ray and I have split up and I stay busy with my new friends. The Wrights never approved of me, so I always keep to myself."

"Do you work?"

"No not anymore."

"How are you living? How do you pay your bills?"

"I only have utilities, car insurance, and food. My house and car are paid for. Ray is giving me money to live on."

The detectives glance at each other. The same Ray she put out of the house is voluntarily giving her money to live on? It didn't smell right.

"So, you have moved on, and made new friends."

"Yes, I have joined a book club."

"We are going to need for you to write down the names of your friends, for character references."

They push a pad and pen towards her. Brenda blushes bright red and bites her lip.

"Guys, Look, I really don't have any friends yet. I mean, I joined the book club but I never went to one meeting. I had every intention but I didn't go. I never met any of the members. I wanted to but I've been very depressed, and just couldn't get the energy to go. I don't have one name to write on that pad."

"Have you talked to anyone, like a doctor or therapist about your sadness?"

"No. I don't have insurance, so I can't see a doctor. I just stay home and watch television. I don't go out a lot."

"There is help out there Brenda. You should contact the health department and see if they have any programs for depression. "Detective Nugent offered. "But lying to us is not going to help with this investigation, Brenda."

Brenda shrugs her shoulders.

"What kind of television shows do you watch?" Detective Tope asks her.

Brenda looks panicked. Her eyes widen, and she looks guilty. "I, um, I don't really watch the shows, I really just have the television on for noise, so it is not so quiet in the house. I think it is a soap opera, I'm not sure. Maybe game shows sometimes?"

The detectives tell her she can leave but that they will need more information from her, so, "don't leave town." She agrees.

They go one floor down, to the cell where Ray is being held. He is stretched out peacefully on the bunk.

"Hello, boys. I figured you would get to me eventually. Can I get a cigarette from you?"

"Sorry sir, we don't smoke." Detective Nugent said.

"Dang shame. Hey, I saw the coroner's car there at my folk's house, so I can only assume the worst."

"Yes, the worst." Detective Tope said.

Ray just shakes his head. He does not go crazy. He is already crazy. He is silent for about 3 minutes. The detectives were giving him time to process the information.

The detectives size him up. The guy is huge. There is no way he is naturally that muscular. Obviously, he is juiced up with steroids. It would make any man envious except for the knowledge that steroids shrink up your manhood. No man is envious of that.

They leave Ray in the cell and sit at a table outside of the cell.

They begin the interview. Detective Tope turns on the recorder.

"Sir please state your name for the record."

"Ray Wright."

"Your address."

"1542 Esmond Road."

"Are you currently married?"

"I'm separated."

"Wife's name?"

"Brenda Louisa Wright."

"Are you employed?"

"I am a personal trainer at Walley's Hard Bodies Gym"

"Do you work full-time Ray?"

"What in the hell does this have to do with what happened to my folks?"

"We just have to get background information Ray. Please answer the question."

"No. I work about 3, maybe 4 days a week."

The detectives know there is no way Ray can support himself and his estranged wife on 4 days of personal trainer employment.

"Ray, when was the last time you saw your parents alive?"

"Yesterday. My dad called me and said that my son, Glenn, who lives with them, had stolen some of his checks and had also taken his car without his permission. He told me he was pressing charges this time. We had a few words. I went over there. Mom got in between us. I left mad. Glenn already has a messed-up life. I didn't understand how Pops could threaten to put him back in jail."

"Their car is at the house now."

"Yeah."

"So, Glenn didn't take the car?"

"I don't think so. He didn't want to upset Pops."

"There is no sign of Glenn. Could he have murdered them?"

Ray's face reddened and he immediately screams, "No! He's a junkie, a thief, and a bum, not a killer. He wouldn't hurt a fly. He is a good kid. He has just had a run of bad luck. He got set up by a wetback undercover cop and went down for drugs he didn't even have on him. They planted them on him." Ray was screaming at the top of his lungs and beating on his own chest. In his anger, he grabs the cell bars and attempts to shake them. The bars are iron, so he is not able to move them. He turned violent so quickly that it took the detectives by surprise. It was all they could do not jump or react to his over-the-top outburst. However, they remain calm. This outburst is a classic symptom of what is called Roid Rage, or Steroid Rage.

The detective's secretary Madge buzzes in. They walk out to see what she wants and leave Ray to his temper tantrum. In the back of their minds, they both know the Wrights would not be able to defend themselves from that kind of rage.

They meet with Madge in their office.

"I have the information you asked for regarding the Wright House. Dispatch has a record of 70 calls to this residence in 3 years with no charges pressed. Also, Mr. Martin, a neighbor is here to speak to you about the Wrights."

They see Mr. Martin in the small lobby they have on their main floor. It is an informal meeting.

"Hello. I'm Mr. Clay Martin. I live 3 houses to the left of the Wrights. Their grandson Glenn was always screaming at them. I saw him kick the little dog in the air and the dog ran off, howling in pain, and hide under another neighbor's house. Every time I heard the little dog howl, I knew it was being abused. I called the police but Glenn was gone every time they arrived. The police didn't stay long. The dispatcher would call me back and tell me to report it to animal control, which I did. I never heard back from them. I guess the Wrights didn't want to press charges. I just thought you should know. Their Son, he's a huge guy, like 6'6, any time he came over, he was screaming and ranting and raving at them. I felt sorry for them, but anytime I called the police, they refused help so I quit calling." Mr. Martin writes his statement down and signs it. He gives his name, address, and contact number. "I only came forward because I saw you arrest the son. I admit I am afraid of him, afraid of his revenge for me speaking out. I'm old. The grandson is as bad as the father."

The detectives thank him for coming forward and state they will be in touch.

Detective Nugent contacts 911 dispatch and puts out a BOLO (Be On The Look Out) for Glenn Wright, Age 23, Blonde hair, Green eyes, 5'10", 140lbs., tattoos. He also asks Madge to contact Glenn's Probation Officer and ask him to come to their office for a meeting.

They go back to continue interviewing Ray. He is pacing in the cell.

"Look my kid didn't mean no harm. My folks were always riding him. Pressuring him to get a job, but when he used their car to go look for a job, they raised hell. They constantly complained and argued with him. He couldn't do nothing right."

"What do you mean he didn't mean no harm? What did he do?"

"He just yelled back when Pops yelled at him. He was frustrated that's all."

"Well, we just got a statement from a neighbor that the Wrights were afraid of you and their grandson. He said y'all were constantly screaming at them and abusing their little dog."

"Oh, bull crap. That dog is taken better care of than any kid in the world. I hate that little wharf rat. It even sleeps in the bed with them. It's going to the pound as soon as I get out of here."

Detective Nugent smiles at Ray. He thinks Ray is lying to cover his tracks. Ray looks away and says, "Well, don't you think you should let me go? If you had anything on me, you would send me to jail."

"We can keep you up to 36 hours for the investigation Ray." Detective Tope says as he walks out of the room with Detective Nugent. They can hear Ray cursing and screaming his displeasure.

As they enter their office, the telephone on Detective Tope's desk rings. It is the coroner.

"Tope, I think you guys need to get over here. I'm not done, but you should see this."

"Yes sir, we are on our way." and he hangs up.

"What's up?" Detective Nugent asks.

"The coroner wants us to come see some stuff, dead stuff."

"Crap. I'd rather see four hundred dead bodies than one autopsy."

"Yeah, I know the feeling."

Detective Nugent calls dispatch on the telephone and asks for a supervisor. Nettie Sterling comes on the line.

"Hello Nettie, this is Detective Nugent. I hope you are doing great girl! Listen, we have Ray Wright in our holding cell. He is a huge angry man. Probably on steroids. I need you to wait about an hour, then send four officers, big ones, to transport him to the county jail on a hold order. We are not through interviewing him. Tell the officers to use caution. However, if he starts to fight them, tell them to leave his ass in our cell. I don't want anyone to get hurt."

"10-4 Detective. You guys be safe out there."

"Will do Nettie."

Detective Plant rides with Tope and Nugent to the coroner's office.

The Coroner, Sammie Tandem, says, "Greetings" as the detectives enter the room. 3 gurneys hold the 2 human victims and the 1 decapitated dog. Brad Plant enters directly behind them.

"Thanks for coming right over guys. The impact of the injuries is more impressive in person than in photographs. Detective Plant, I will ask you to wait to photograph until after the tour, please. Let us begin with the male."

He pulls the sheet back. A naked Mr. Wright is covered in every color bruise you can imagine. "The rainbow of colors indicates, new and old bruises on the body.

Purple is the newest bruise, green, yellow, and faint white with slight colorization being older. There are (2) 6-inch-diameter purple bruises directly over the left portion of the chest, in layman's terms, directly over the heart. Again, this man took (2) direct hits to his heart. If you look you will see it appears the attacker was wearing gloves, most likely boxing gloves according to the pattern of some of the bruising.

However, we did find a fingerprint and a thumbprint on the back of the man's right bicep that appears to be approximately a week old. X-rays show he has 3 new broken ribs that have recently been broken and 6 older ones that are in the process of healing. He has advanced heart disease that could have been treated with medication, however there is no medication in his system. I did a hair sample test; he hasn't had medication in the past year. If he had, it would have shown in the hair sample. His brain shows signs of being hit in the head, often, there are indications of brain injury. He suffered cognitive damage due to the amount of injuries to his head. I would say he suffered from Dementia also.

There are multiple cigarette burns to his forearms, legs, and the tops of his feet. There is no pattern, so they likely happened at different times. I also found it ironic that his feet are overly calloused."

The coroner shakes his head in disgust, "Both victims are underweight and severely malnourished. Moving on to the female. She has large chunks of hair that have been pulled from the back of her head and bruising on her back, thighs, and buttocks, it is my professional opinion someone was using a belt to strike her. The width of the bruising is consistent with 2 inches. She also has a smaller handprint bruise on her mouth and a broken partial, as if the partial was slapped out of her mouth. There are multicolor bruises on her wrists and ankles consistent with being restrained. Her nails were cut, but I am still testing for skin cells, I will let you know. God, I hope you catch the monster who did this."

Detective Nugent sighs. "We do too. And the dog?"

The coroner shakes his head, "You know as bad as it sounds, I have dogs at home, they are like my kids. This one hurts my heart the most. I deal with dead bodies 6 and 7 days a week. This little dog had been starved and beaten to death before he was decapitated. His skull has been hit so many times that he developed tumors on his little brain. I am sure he had seizures daily. He was tortured too. His neck has been stretched almost 7 inches, which means he was hung at some point while he was alive. He had blood in his mouth and under his nails so he may have bitten or scratched his attacker trying to get away from him at a previous time or it may be that he bit and scratched himself not knowing what he was doing. I extracted the blood from his teeth and nails. I will send the results to the crime lab when I get them."

Detective Plant says, "I need to take the pictures for the case file."

Dispatch radios the detectives to tell them Glenn Wright's Probation Officer is in their office. The others tell Detective Plant they will send Patrol to drive him back to his car so he can stay and take photographs. He gives them a dirty look but says, "Okay fine." He hates the morgue as much as any of them.

They go back to the office and meet with Senior Probation Officer, Horace Melan. Detective Nugent offers him a cup of coffee. He accepts.

"Horace, tell us about Glenn Wright. I don't know if you know but his grandparents were found murdered."

"No, I hadn't heard that. I am truly sorry to hear that."

Detective Tope notices Horace Melan looks like a guilty man. He has dark circles under his eyes,

his hair is mussed, and his clothing is unkempt. He has a slight tremor as he is handed the coffee.

" Listen guys, I need to be transparent with you. We are shorthanded at the Probation office. I've

single-handedly got 85 cases that I'm carrying right now. I'm on the brink of a nervous

breakdown. The secretaries keep quitting because we are putting too much pressure and way too

much responsibility on them. I'm behind on my notes and my visitations because I'm constantly

in court with new probationers pouring into our system."

Detectives Nugent and Tope are dumbfounded.

Tope asks, "Do you know Glenn Wright? Have you met him? He is supposed to be under house

arrest."

Horace is pale and his brow is covered in sweat. He opens a file folder he brought with him and reads from it. "Glenn Wright is residing at 1313 Marina Coffee Place with his grandparents, Mr. and Mrs. Boyd Wright. He is under house arrest. He calls in weekly to an answering machine to let us know he is okay and drug-free. He mails in $50.00 (fifty dollars) a month for probation fee. That is all the information I have at this time."

"When have you MET with him?' Detective Nugent asks.

"I met with him after sentencing on February 17, 1984. I gave him his instructions then."

Both of the detective's mouths drop open. That is over a year and a half ago that the probation officer has seen Glenn Wright.

"Horace what the hell?" Detective Tope yells.

"Guys, I can't help it! I'm working 6 days a week, 12 and 14 hours a day. I have it on record here

that he calls in weekly for his check-ins. I haven't even been able to do a house check. I haven't

been able to leave the office. I just explained that to you, I'm in court most of the time. There is a

tidal wave of crime that is combatted with Probation. I have begged for help."

"Isn't the monitor supposed to sound an alarm when it is taken off of the offender's ankle?"

"Yes, if it were activated. We have so many that I turned off the machines. I couldn't go and

track down everyone who took the monitors off. We don't have enough jail space for them."

"Why do you stay in that mess Horace?" Detective Nugent asks him.

"I've only got 13 months until I can retire," Horace puts his head down and says softly.

Detective Nugent loses his patience and yells, "Listen! I want you to go right now and charge

Glenn with violation of probation, do you understand me? He is not staying at home under house

arrest. His electronic monitor was found on the ankle of his dead grandmother! He is out driving his grandparent's car whenever he wants. We have a BOLO out for him to question him for his

grandparents' murder. I'm not kidding Horace, go immediately and violate him. Do I make

myself clear?"

Horace shakes his head yes and says, "I'm so sorry guys."

Detective Tope points to the door and Horace walks out, with his head down.

Detective Nugent says, "This job is going to be the death of me, Tope."

They walk over to their holding cell, it is empty, so Ray must have cooperated with the officers.

The detectives sit at their desks and work on their reports. Both men work quietly without

talking. It's been a rough day. They have a daily report that they have to turn in to the supervisor,

Lt. Hearn. It details all the information they have gathered on the daily shift, the people

interviewed and evidence gathered, and then an advanced report they work on daily to be turned

in when the case is solved or deemed unable to be solved.

After they leave for the night, they stop by Michelle's, a cop bar, and have a few drinks. They

need it. Their guts are twisted up like a tornado has hit them. They don't stay long. Tonight even

the liquor is not numbing the horrible feelings they have so they go home early.

The next morning before their first cup of coffee is finished, patrol Sgt. Brown telephones them with news, "Night shift is on the way in. They just picked up Glenn Wright. You want him over there?"

"Yes please." Detective Tope says.

"10-4"

"Thanks, Mike," Tope says and hangs up the telephone. "Nugent, that was Mike Brown, they

picked up, Glenn Wright."

"Fanfreakingtastic."

Detective Plant walks in with his camera. "Heard on the radio they got Glenn Wright. I'm here to

get pictures of his arms, legs, face, hands, fingers, and toes."

"Thanks, man. You saved me a phone call." Nugent says. "Have patrol hold him down while you

photograph him in case, he is wild and wooly like his daddy."

"I will if I need to, but I gotta feeling he only beats up old folks." Plant responds grimly. "I've

got some pictures for you two. They are pretty bad. I will be finished at lunch."

Detectives Nugent and Tope go back out into the neighborhood of the Wrights to attempt to

question the neighbors. This morning the neighbors are more willing to cooperate since they

heard on the news that the son and grandson are in jail.

Mr. Michael Page, 1412 Marina Coffee Place, age 72 states that he grows prize-winning roses on

his property and many times, Angus, the Wright's poodle would dig under his fence, urinate on

his roses, and attack the roses. Then he would run into the backyard, run in circles like he was

crazy, and then attack the vegetable garden. He caught the dog eating his vegetables. This

enraged Mr. Page. He called the police 25 times between March 17 and September 14, to report.

The police would not press charges. He was told it was a civil matter.

Anna Bell, who resides at 1417 Marina Coffee Plaza, heard a UPS man screaming at Mrs. Wright

on Friday morning, for not opening the door to take possession of a package. The driver was

cursing and screaming, beating on the door and windows.

"You are causing me to run late lady. I need to deliver 40 other packages. This is the 3rd time I

have been here today. The car is here so I know someone is home. I am sick and tired of

babysitting these freaking packages for you and your husband just because you are old as dirt,"

"Mrs. Wright opened the door just a little bit, like she was scared, and the UPS driver pushed the

door open and was standing over her, bullying her and still screaming at her. He shoved the

machine at her for her to sign for the package, then he threw the box into her house and stormed

off into his delivery truck. I witnessed all of this. I was walking my dog, Ranger, when this

happened." The detectives thanked her for the information and gave her their card in case she

remembered anything else.

The detectives have dispatch find out the driver's information from UPS. They go straight to the

UPS office and the supervisor calls, Jose Rivers, the driver, into the homicide office, off of his

route. He was humbled by then, stating he was stressed out, it was only his 5th day on the job and

he is truly sorry for being rude to the elderly lady. He has just moved there from Florida. NCIC revealed he had a 4-time history of Felony Family Violence Charges. He was fired from UPS,

and he was taken into custody for more questioning at the Homicide division. The detectives

decided not to charge him for crimes against the elderly since their victim was dead.

Once back in the car, Detective Nugent said, "Tope what kind of feeling do you get about Jose Rivers?"

Tope said, "I honestly think he is just a punk that likes pushing women around. I don't see him

killing the Wrights. I just wanted to bring him in to rattle his cage. Maybe we should put him in

the cell with Ray and let them go 9 rounds."

Detective Nugent laughs and says, "My money would be on Ray, that's for sure."

Dispatched interrupts their conversation. "Homicide detectives, go to Channel 6 please."

They turn off the main channel on the radio and go to channel 6. "Go ahead dispatch."

"Just wanted to let you know that your suspect Jose Rivers is using an alias, his real name is

Miguel San Michael. We learned it from NCIC and he is using his cousin's social security

number. He has warrants for acts of Felony Family Violence out of Bay County Florida. We are

placing a hold on him for Florida."

"That's 10-4 dispatch. Will you please ask Lieutenant Haney to contact us?"

The Lieutenant is already on the line, "Go to channel 6 Nugent."

On channel 6, Detective Nugent asks, "Sir, do you want to charge Miguel San Michael with giving false information or do you just want Florida to be advised we have him?"

The Lieutenant states, "He has to have an extradition hearing to have Florida come pick him up.

Just release him to Florida. Tell him if he fights it we will charge him with our own charges and

then turn him over to Florida after he has served his time here."

"Thanks, Lt."

The detectives look at each other and grin. "Another good call."

They stop and have lunch. Neither has much of an appetite, but they know they need to eat.

Running on coffee and junk food can cloud your judgment and make you sluggish when you

need to be sharp. They eat in silence. The last 2 days have been ridiculously tough.

After lunch, they hear back from dispatch. "Could you return to your office, please? Detective

Plant needs to meet with you."

Detective Plant is waiting for them. They go into the conference room. He hands them each 50

pictures of the crime scene.

Detective Tope begins. He looks at a photo and then passes it to Nugent, who either puts it in a

stack on the table or pins it to the evidence board. The first picture is an empty refrigerator. It is

clean and completely empty. It is a story all its own. It's haunting. How were the elderly people

being fed if there was no food? There is also no food in the kitchen cabinets. Not even a cracker.

This made both detectives feel sick especially since they had just had lunch.

The second picture is the bed with no sheets or blankets. The room that this mattress is in, has a

padlock on the outside of the door. The mattress has blood and urine stains on it. There are also

cigarette burns on it. These pictures are pinned to the evidence board.

Detective Plant goes on to explain there is not one pair of shoes in the entire house and he hands the detectives pictures of the victim's feet which are covered in heavy calluses. They remember the coroner showing them both victims' feet were heavily callused.

"Ray or Glenn probably took away the shoes to keep them from running away." Detective Plant says.

There is no clothing for the victims except for pajamas, and they are threadbare from being worn

repeatedly. There also is no medication for either victim.

There is a stack of overdue credit card bills, that were hidden in a drawer that had a false bottom

of a drawer, the invoices are in the victim's name and there is an eviction notice.

Plant is an excellent photographer, no doubt. He discovers that the partial print near the body was tampered with purposely so it could not be identified, however, he was able to measure how big half of the shoe was. He also has pictures of 8 different cigarette butts that were located outside in the yard. He gathers them for evidence. No cigarettes were found inside the house. An ashtray has been emptied, and wiped clean, the garbage has been removed. The detectives were able to use 40 pictures for the evidence board and Plant still has to develop the autopsy photographs.

Detective Nugent says, "You know Plant, I think I want you to go with us to Ray's wife's house and take some photos there."

"10-4 let me know when"

"In the afternoon tomorrow. Let's surprise her."

The detectives return to interview Glenn Wright.

When they arrived, Glenn Wright is slouching down on the bench his father had been sitting on

24 hours earlier. He reeks of dirty sweat and crack cocaine. His blonde hair is slicked to the left

side of his head, but it stands up in the back. He has a slight beard, not because he didn't shave.

He doesn't have the balls to grow a real beard. There are just patches of hair, here and there. The

detectives are not impressed by what they see.

He is not muscled up like his father. It is quite the opposite; Skinny Glenn Wright jumps up when

they enter the room, he is nervous, sweating, and paranoid.

The patrol officers who picked him up said they caught him trying to break into the Wrights'

residence. Detective Tope decides to interview Glenn through the bars of the cell. Mainly

because they thought they might beat him to a pulp if they determined it was him who tortured

his grandparents. Detective Plant snaps a few pictures of him in his current state. It is raining

torrential rain outside and a huge boom of thunder hits. Glenn nearly jumps out of his skin.

The detectives smile and turn on the recorder.

"I'm Detective Tope and this is Detective Nugent. Please state your name for the recorder."

"Glenn Wright. What is happening? What is that sound?"

"What are you talking about Glenn?" Detective Nugent decides to mess with his mind for a second. "Do you know why you were brought here?"

"You caught me trying to take the car? Do you think I robbed a bank? You think I stole something?"

"No."

The lightning and thunder strike again. This time Glenn recognizes the sound. He starts rubbing his neck, and then his hands together.

"When was the last time you saw Boyd and Agnes Wright?"

"Who?"

"Your grandparents you twit!" Detective Nugent snapped.

Detective Tope covers his face, trying not to laugh, and points to the recorder. Nugent turns away to collect himself.

"Again, when was the last time you saw them?"

"A couple of days ago, I think., Gramps loaned me his car."

"What kind of relationship do you have with them?"

"It's okay. I mean they are pretty uptight. They don't like my friends, my music, or nothing about me."

"We heard you were in jail."

"Yeah, I was set up. Some rookie cop said I tried to buy dope from him. The judge gave me 2

years but my old man got it fixed where I could stay with Gramps. I only served 2 months. The

rest is house arrest."

"Do you have any idea where your ankle monitor is?"

Glenn gets a stupid look on his face and says, "What?"

At that moment, Detective Rachel Rivera from Financial Crimes comes in and asks to speak to

the detectives. They leave Glenn and go back to the office. She has a large envelope for each of

them.

"I received these from the Wrights bank. Your boy here has stolen 35 checks from the Wrights.

The total of checks cashed is ($5417.00) Five thousand four hundred seventeen dollars and zero

cents. All of the checks were made out to cash and cashed at Ripley's Spirits and Liquor Store.

This account has not been accessed in years. Apparently, Glenn Wright stumbled upon some

checks and got busy with them.

Boyd Wright had slipped a handwritten note to the mailman with no stamp asking for his help to

report the theft and asking for help. The liquor store had Glenn on video-cashing all of the

checks. We have the videos at the liquor store. The mailman delivered the note to the bank. The

bank contacted us. We contacted the Department of Family and Children's Services and we were

getting ready to arrest Glenn Wright for the stolen checks when we heard the murders took

place."

The detectives thank Detective Rivera for her help. She shakes her head, "This POS is a

monster."

Detectives Tope and Nugent go back to Glenn Wright. He is sitting up on the bench, snoring.

Nugent takes a tin cup and runs it back and forth on the steel bars loud enough to stir Glenn.

"Wake up dude, we need more information."

"Bout what? Leave me alone asshole!" an angry Glenn screams.

"Boyd and Agnes Wright." Detective Top says.

"Who?"

"Your grandparents for God's sake!" Detective Tope screams.

"Piss off! "Glenn sits up straighter, then bends over, and holds his head in his hands. "Where am

I?"

"You are in a holding cell in the Homicide Division of the Police Department."

Look, man. I need some sleep. I can't think. I have been awake for days."

Tope turns off the recorder and says, "Look you little bastard, we need answers. Did you do that

to your grandparents?"

Glenn lays face down on the bench, passes gas loudly, and then begins snoring loudly.

The detectives are furious. They storm out and Detective Tope calls for a patrol unit to transport

Glenn to the jail. They give orders that Glenn and Ray not be near each other in the jail and to

bag Glenn's clothing and shoes for evidence. Detective Nugent calls Financial Crimes and tells

Detective Rivera, she can go ahead with her charges against Glenn.

The detectives type up the beginning of their reports on the computer and save it. Their daily

report they turn in to their supervisor, Lt. Haney to explain the progress.

Once the detectives arrive at their perspective homes, they have no idea they have the same

routines. Walking through the door their jackets come off, they remove their ties, they each pour 3 fingers of bourbon, then they plop down into their recliners, and kick off their shoes.

Each falls asleep in front of the television, though they never watch anything. It is on just to

drown out the noise in their heads. Around midnight, they wake up and take a shower, then get

into bed. Up again at 5 am. Both sleep restlessly; images of Mr. and Mrs. Wright in their minds,

that they can't unsee. Actual proof that monsters exist. Detective Plant's photographs help to

intensify their nightmares.

The next morning, Detective Tope wakes up early and goes into the office to go over the

interview tapes. He is just getting his 2nd cup of coffee when Detective Nugent comes in.

"Morning bud. You get any sleep?"

Detective Tope shakes his head and says, "Probably about as much as you did."

Detective Plant comes in and says, "I got some great pictures of Ray and Glenn Wright. Patrol is

transporting Glenn Wright over to you in about 20 minutes. His Highness is eating his breakfast

and the jail won't transport him during that time. I will have those pictures developed by tomorrow morning. What time are we going to the wife's?"

"About 1 pm. We want to interview Glenn first."

"Okey Dokey, I will follow you this time in my car so you don't leave me stranded again."

The already aggravated Detectives don't say anything, they just grunt. They hate the politics

that come with the job. Yes, everyone is presumed innocent until proven guilty but they don't

see why they have to kiss the county jail's butt every time they request a prisoner. The new

sheriff is a real stickler for inmate's rights.

When Plant leaves, the office is quiet as each of them prepares mentally for the day ahead.

Detective Tope pours over the financial statements and Detective Nugent examines the

neighbor's testimonies.

Madge, their secretary comes in and says there is a message on the answering machine that she is

forwarding to Detective Tope's telephone.

The Detectives hate getting bad news so early in the morning, it kind of sets the tone for the

entire day, but Detective Tope sighs and puts the call on speakerphone so they both can hear it.

An elderly woman's voice came on the answering machine.

"Hello. This is Daisy Porter. I live near the Wrights house. I was scared to talk to you so I didn't answer my door when you came by. I apologize. But once I knew the son was in jail, I knew I should call you. I wanted to tell you; that the most horrible screams came from that house at night mainly. The son drove a big truck, I don't know what kind, but every time it was there, there was chaos. I saw the son hit his father's head on the truck hood one time when I was walking. I walk because of my cholesterol, kind of doctor's orders. Anyhow the son ran after me that day and said his father fell and hit his head. I know what I saw. That poor old man's head bounced off of the hood of that black truck. I saw it. Maybe my face said something different, so the man threatened me and said to mind my own business or he would pay me a visit. He told me he knew where I lived. I ran all the way home. I hope this helps." Then the line went dead.

Detective Tope asked Madge to get Dispatch to send them a copy of the 911 call alerting them to

the murders. He wants to compare the voices to see if she was the one who called in the murder.

In a few minutes, Patrol arrives and has Glenn Wright with them. Officer Bob asks, "Where do

y'all want him?"

Detective Nugent calls out from his office, "Put him in the cell. Thanks."

Detective Plant has already taken more pictures of a cleaned-up version of Glenn.

The detectives take their time and have another cup of coffee. They want Glenn to be unsure of himself. Waiting sometimes makes people impatient and unpredictable. It also makes crackheads

a little more paranoid. Glenn might give them more information if he is unsettled.

The detectives read over some of the coroner's report. It would hurt the hardest heart to see the

torture these 2 victims endured.

"Well, let's go get some quality time with the dear boy." Detective Nugent says.

Detective Tope shakes his head in disgust.

They observe Glenn through the 2-way mirror.

He has showered and is wearing an orange, county jail jumpsuit. His hair is clean, his teeth

brushed, and his pathetic baby beard is gone. He looks younger than his 23 years. In some way,

he doesn't look like the same filthy crackhead they had met the night before. Tope is thinking, "If

only the Judges could see them like they are when we first get them, it might strengthen their sentences."

Detective Nugent turns on the recorder.

"State your name for the record."

"Glenn Wright."

"Glenn, I'm Detective Nugent and this is Detective Tope. We are investigating the murder of

Boyd and Agnes Wright."

When asked why he has his arms inside his shirt, he complains he is cold.

"Glenn, did you kill your grandparents?"

"No."

Detective Tope notices Glenn looks away when he answers. After many years of training and experience the detectives know this is a sign of dishonesty or deception.

"Did you inflict injury on them in any way?"

"Ummm. I might have hurt their feelings. We were always yelling, and screaming at each other,

but I never touched them. Pops has a loud booming voice. He can't talk to nobody, he always has

to scream and belittle folks."

"Do you know who would hurt them?"

"Nope." (He looks away again.)

"Glenn, I have to ask you again, did you ever strike your grandfather?"

"No, um, once when he was pushing me, trying to stop me from leaving in his car, I pushed him

away from me but he didn't fall. He only stumbled."

"Why didn't he want you to drive his car?"

"He was a selfish old bast… selfish old man."

"Glenn why was your grandmother, Agnes Wright, wearing your ankle monitor."

Glenn's face turns bright red and he says, "I don't know what you are talking about."

"Do you have a job, Glenn?"

"I've been looking but nobody is hiring."

"Have you ever had a job?"

"Well, um, my job now is to look after my grandparents."

"I mean before. What was your job before?"

"What does this have to do with anything?"

"We are just gathering background information for the investigation."

"I worked at Pops dealership helping my dad," Glenn says, looking away.

Detective Nugent turns off the recorder. Glenn starts pacing the room. He is sweating and says he feels sick.

The detectives hear a knock at the door and can see it is Detective Plant. They step outside to

meet with him. He has the pictures of Glenn's hands and arms. They are covered with scratches

and bruises. There is also a dog bite on his right calf.

They return to their desk to give Glenn a few minutes to lie down.

Dispatch telephones Detective Nugent and tells him that 2 men have just been arrested for

entering the Wrights residence. They are charged with Burglary and Breaking and Entering a

crime scene.

"Tell the jail to process them and hold them downstairs until we can get over there and interview

them. Put them in separate rooms please."

They return to Glenn.

"Have you thought of any more information that can assist us in this investigation?"

"No."

"What kind of relationship did your father have with the Wrights?"

"Ask him. I don't know. They were HIS parents."

"No Glenn, we are asking you."

"Pops didn't like anybody. He cussed us all out. He didn't appreciate anyone or anything."

"Did Ray get along with Agnes?"

"Yeah, I think he was upset with her for not speaking up for him when he was growing up cause

his old man was a bully. But in today's world, they didn't talk much."

"Okay, Glenn. We are going to transport you back to the jail. We are not through interviewing

you but we have to be somewhere." The detectives handcuff Glenn and transport him back to the

county jail. He is nervous in the back of the detective's car.

"So, um, you guys can let me go. I have told you everything I know." Glenn says with a nervous laugh.

Detective Tope says, "We have not even begun to interview you, Glenn. Be patient with us."

"Patient with you? I'm the one sitting in jail." He says, suddenly angry.

"Yes, but see Glenn. All of this time you were supposed to be under house arrest, you were

driving around in your grandfather's car, while grandma was wearing your ankle monitor. That is

a direct violation of probation. You will probably get 2 years of jail time for that, maybe more,

and if I find out you haven't been completely honest with us about anything, I will press further

charges against you for Purgery. That is lying to the Police. It is against the law."

Glenn is silent for the rest of the 3-minute trip to the county jail.

The arresting officers of Frank Johnson and Junior Hayes are still at the jail when the detectives

arrive. The correctional officer takes Glenn and moves him to the floor he is assigned to..

"Hey, Petri, how's it going?" Detective Tope asks.

"Oh, you know, beating these mean streets. We put Johnson and Hayes in separate interview rooms for you. It's gonna take a month to get that stench out of my car. I think one of them

defecated on himself when we arrested him. Plus, he reeks of crack cocaine, which is really popular on the streets now because it is so cheap and it smells like filth. These idiots can get high

on one crack rock that only costs $10.00. So many people are strung out on it.

It's really bad out here. Robberies, Burglaries, and Thefts have tripled in the past 8 months.

These junkies will do anything to get money. It's pretty sad."

Detective Nugent says, "Yeah, the world is a bad place, Petri. Thank you for working the streets

and trying to make it better. We will see you guys later."

Detective Nugent liked Officer Petri and hoped he would get promoted to Homicide. He was

honest and hard-working. There are not too many dedicated officers anymore. He makes a note

to speak to his Lieutenant about Petri. Hopefully, they can recruit him to Homicide.

Frank Johnson is sitting in a small interview room. He is bald with a red and gray goatee. He is

dirty with that all-familiar smell of crack cocaine. Detective Nugent walks in to meet him. The

smell nearly knocks him down... that rank smell of defecation. He thinks to himself, 'Oh no. Just

my lousy luck, I get the guy with crap in his pants.'

"Hello, Frank. I'm Detective Nugent from Homicide."

"Homicide? What do you want with me?"

"Glenn Wright or Ray Wright? Who is your friend?"

"I don't know who you are talking about."

"Listen, there is only going to be ONE deal made here. Either you can make it or Junior Hayes

can make it. It doesn't matter to me. You both broke into a crime scene, which is a felony so you both will get prison time. If you know something about the Wrights, the victims, you probably

want to share with me right now because when I walk out that door, there will be no deal."

Frank Johnson drops his head and does not answer. He's been around the streets long enough to

know; you just don't give the cops any information on anybody else. Detective Nugent stands up

slowly and then walks out. He takes a couple of deep breaths trying to get that stench out of his

lungs.

He finds a supervisor in the jail; and says, "Yall are going to have to shower Frank Johnson. He

smells disgusting. He crapped himself."

The supervisor says, "Yes sir, the arresting officer warned us. Thanks for the reminder."

2 Correctional Officers go and escort Johnson to the shower. For appearance's sake, Frank puts

up a little fight. The correctional officers strip him and turn the high-powered hose on him. Frank

wasn't counting on that or he would have behaved himself. He starts screaming like a girl

because the power of the water stings. The officer uses this method when people refuse to

shower or are fighting them about showering.. They double-bag his clothing and take them to the

dumpster.

Detective Nugent and the jail supervisor watch the entire thing.

The supervisor says, "Nugent, I bet you a dollar, the next time he comes to jail, he volunteers to

take a shower. " Detective Nugent whistles and says, "A whole dollar? That's pretty high stakes for a dirty bag like that! Make it a nickel and you got yourself a bet." They laugh.

The other suspect, Junior Hayes is young, maybe 25 years old. He is very skinny, has a black mohawk, is covered in tattoos, and is about 5'3". He is sweating like a pig when Detective Tope walks in.

"Hello, Junior. I'm Detective Tope from Homicide. I came in here to offer you a deal. My partner

is right now offering the same deal to Frank Johnson. Whoever agrees to the deal first gets it. Do

you understand?"

"What's the deal? What is this about?"

"We will talk to the judge and get you probation for these 2 charges you came in on. But you

have to be straight with us. It will take about 3 days to get you out of here but if you give me

what I need, you will get out on Probation."

"What do you want?"

"We need to know about Ray and Glenn Wright."

Junior's eyes are blank for a minute, then they get wide. He thinks for a minute, and he is still

sweating. The smell is revolting, and crack is pouring through his skin, but Detective Tope

toughs it out. He has a feeling Junior is ready to talk. The young man's face looks mournful and

distraught.

"Junior, I need answers. You are pretty small to go to prison. Do you know what they do to small guys in prison? They make girlfriends out of them. Its really kind of sad. The prison officers don't do anything to protect the small guys. This is the only way to help yourself stay out of prison. It is a felony to break in to a crime scene and your broke in to a murder scene. So I think you should tell me about Ray and Glenn and the Wrights."

Junior clears his throat and scratches his head. He has lice. Dective Tope can see them flying around his head. He feels bad for Junior for a minute, but he backs up so none of those bugs jump on him.

"You not lying about that deal right? I mean if I tell you I need protection."

"I am a man of my word Junior. Tell me what you know."

"Ray, um, that's Glenn's dad, um, he hired me and Frank to do some work on the yard. We were

walking by their house one day. He hollered at us to come here for a minute and asks if we could

mow his lawn and rake it for $30.00. We said, "Hell yeah." He says the landlord has been

complaining and he says he didn't have time to take care of it. Me and Frank, we stole a lawn

mower and 2 rakes and clean up the yard real nice. Ray and Glenn are not home while we were

working. I told Frank that I could hear somebody beating on the window and the door. Frank

walked over to the window and somebody was yelling for help. Frank laughed at them.

I guess they locked them inside when Ray and Glenn were gone. It was kinda creepy.

After we finish the yard, Glenn comes back with some rocks (crack) and tells us to come in and party with him.

"Is this enough information?" he asks Detective Tope, hopefully.

"Not even close." Detective Tope says, shaking his head no.

Junior sighs, and his eyes tear up. "Well, we partied. Glenn had some whiskey and we smoked the crack rocks. We were pretty messed up. Glenn tells us that his grandparents are locked in their room because they will not tell him where the safe is at."

Frank asks, "What safe?"

"He, Glenn, says there is a safe full of money and gold coins, hidden in this house. He says if we can make them talk there is a huge reward. He says he will give us half. Frank gets excited and tells him we can make them talk. I was really messed up...Glenn, um, he unlocks the padlock on the door and there were these 2 old people. We scream at them, demanding they tell us where the safe was hidden. Frank pushes them around.

Frank also put a pillowcase over the old man's head and spins him around while screaming at him, 'Where is the safe?'"

"What were you doing while this was happening?"

"I am so messed up. I am sitting on the bed crying, I'm so freaked out, and I'm squeezing a pillow or a dog. I can't remember.

The old man is confused and starts to cry. Frank grabs the woman and snatches a couple of

handfuls of hair from her head, walking her around the room on her tippy toes, and screaming at her. Then, I think the old man takes a swing at Frank, you know trying to defend the woman, and then Frank, he lands 3 or 4 good punches to the old man's side. Frank looks so serious and he is screaming, "Where is the safe old man?" Franks eyes are bugging out of his head. I get scared. Frank looks evil when he gets that angry. He is desperate for that money in the safe.

Suddenly, we hear laughing and we realize we have been had when we look at the door and Glenn is there laughing hysterically. I never touched either of them. It was all Frank. Ray comes home and him and Glenn have words about him having company, but after he smokes a crack rock, Ray calms down and they laugh together. Ray never paid us for the yard work. We stole the lawn mower for nothing. He run us off. Saying don't come back or he will kick our asses. He wouldn't even let us have the lawnmower or the rakes."

"Is there anything else?"

"No sir. I'm ashamed I was around that. I hope you can protect me in jail. Frank will kill me if he finds out I snitched. If he don't, Ray or Glenn will when they find out I told ya."

"Just one more question. Why did you go back there, today?"

"We needed a place to crash. We been high for days. We heard about the murder, so we watched the house from those woods across the street, and no one had been there except a woman. I think she was just a nosey neighbor she was peeking in windows."

"What did she look like?"

"Fat, old, white hair."

Detective Tope tells Junior, "I will keep my word about the deal. However, you may have to

testify in court if we need you."

Junior drops his head and says, "Just promise to protect me."

The detectives speak to the Warden of the jail and ask to have Junior transferred to a jail in a nearby county for his safety until they can get him on probation. The warden agrees. The detectives leave the jail and go back to their office.

After meeting with the Lieutenant, they go to lunch, and though neither of them is hungry, they

force themselves to eat.

After lunch they have Ray Wright transported from the jail to the cell in their office.

"You look well rested Ray." Detective Tope says. There is bitterness in his tone.

"Yep, sleeping good, eating good."

"Well, the taxpayers do their best." Detective Nugent said, sarcastically. Then he turned on the recorder.

"State your name for the record."

"Ray Wright."

"Ray, tell me about Frank Johnson and Junior Hayes."

"Don't know them," Ray says with a smirk on his face.

"Ray take a second. Think about this, before you answer a second time."

Ray shrugged his shoulders, "Oh you mean the lawn company I hired to do the yard. Yes, they

cut the grass and raked the yard. I highly recommend them."

"Were they friends with Glenn?"

"No, I got their number off of their truck. Complete strangers."

Detective Nugent smiles at Ray. Not in a friendly way, but in an, I caught you in a lie, way. Ray

looks at him and wonders what that smile means.

Detective Tope comes in and plays the tape of Junior Hayes interview.

They omit Junior's name and play the part of the confession. Ray has a blank, stunned look on

his face but does not speak.

Suddenly he becomes enraged. He screams, "That is a damnable lie. They worked for my father."

Detective Nugent calmly says, "You are getting confused Ray. You said you hired them."

"I, I don't care. Glenn would never let anyone hurt my folks."

"Ray, we have only just begun to lean on them. I'm sure they have more to give us. Now is the

time to share your truth."

Detective Nugent turns off the tape recorder.

Ray screams, "I don't have anything to confess. I know my rights."

Detective Tope slams his hand down on the desk and screams," If you can name 3 of your rights,

I will let you go right now!"

Ray is dumbfounded. He can't think of one of his rights.

Detective Tope laughs and says, "Ray, I truly think you and your son Glenn are good for these murders. I want to remind you that the state of Washington is a capital punishment state. That

means if we can prove you are guilty, it's the gas chamber for both of you."

Ray rages again, "You have nothing on me. You have to let me go. This is kidnapping. Leave my

kid alone. He didn't do nothing neither." He begins pacing and cursing.

Detective Nugent sighs and turns to Detective Tope, "I know... it's my turn."

He unlocks the door and steps into the cell with Ray. Ray rushes him and punches him twice in

his face, then once in his stomach. He tries to turn him around and get Detective Nugent in a

chokehold but ultimately he fails when Detective Tope comes from behind and hits him over the

head with a long, black flashlight.

It knocks Ray out cold. When Ray comes to, he learns he is charged with Aggravated Assault on a Law Enforcement Officer, A Felony.

There is a detailed incident report written up explaining the event for the supervisor. The

Lieutenant comes by to check on Detective Nugent.

"He gotcha pretty good. You gonna have yourself quite a shiner there boy."

"Yes sir. He is a big guy. I can't believe I let him get the jump on me, but I guess it happens."

Detective Tope laughs and points at Detective Nugent and says, "Oh, he will be okay. His face

didn't have any business being that purdy before he got beat up."

They all laugh as Detective Nugent rubs his jaw.

The Lieutenant says, "Sometimes we gotta take one for the team son. I'm glad you are okay. I hope Tope didn't let him get too many punches in before stepping in." And he laughs again.

"Tope, buy him lunch tomorrow." The Lieutenant says as he walks out.

"But it was his turn." Detective Tope protests. They all laugh.

———————————

The detectives finally drive to Brenda's house. It is a very nice house on the outside. Probably worth $75,000 or 80,000 dollars. It is brick, with a circular driveway, beautiful plants, and a double wood and glass door. It is extremely impressive.

"Hey Nugent, distract her while I look, okay?" Tope asks.

"Yep. I could use the rest." He says sarcastically. He rubs his face again.

When Brenda answers the door, she looks shocked.

"I, uh, I wasn't expecting you. Can you please come back? The house is a mess. I've been, uh,

I've been sick," Brenda says.

"No ma'am we need to speak to you now." Detective Tope says.

Everyone turns around as Detective Plant drives up fast into the driveway. He is there to take

pictures of Brenda's house.

"Who is that?" Brenda asks nervously.

"Oh, he is with us." Detective Tope explains. "Excuse his driving. He thinks he is a racecar driver."

Brenda ignores the joke and looks pitiful. Detective Nugent feels a sense of pity for her.

"Brenda, we have a warrant to come in and take a look around. You are not in any kind of

trouble. All of this is just part of the investigation."

After hearing the word warrant and seeing the paper in Detective Tope's hand, she steps back and allows them to enter.

"Looks like you got hurt detective. Are you okay?" Brenda asks.

"Yes, thank you for your concern. Just another unsatisfied criminal. It happens."

The inside of Brenda's house is disgusting. The smell is repulsive There is old garbage piled

high. The sink is overrun with dirty dishes. Dirty laundry is stacked high in the laundry room.

Old wine bottles line up on the dining room table.

Since Detective Nugent has her distracted, Detective Plant takes a few bags of trash to the back

room and photographs the contents.

Detective Nugent sits with Brenda in the living room and says, "Brenda it is not unusual for

depressed persons not to clean their houses. It is a symptom of the depression. However, I will

tell you this, you will feel so much better if you clean up the house. I strongly suggest you do

that to help yourself. This is a lovely house. I was very surprised when we pulled up."

Brenda is drinking wine. She smiles and says, "Thanks, we bought it when times were good."

"Have you remembered anything that could help us solve the Wrights murder?"

"No sir. I have no idea who would hurt them."

He looks at her and she blushes bright red. He knows he affects her. That blushing is a trait that

her son Glenn inherited from her.

Detective Nugent looks around the room and notices the television is on and Law and Order is

playing. He has a voice activated tape recorder in his pocket and forgets to tell her. He is a little unstable as her husband had hit him with some pretty hard blows to the head.

"Brenda, where did you work before?"

Brenda takes a sip of her wine and says "I, uh, I was the financial adviser and financial manager

for Boyd Ford Motors. I started with them before I met Ray and stayed with them until almost

the end. I began as a personal secretary for Boyd Wright. God, he was horrible. He screamed all

the time. Mrs. Boyd was always a nervous wreck. She was sweet though. She remembered our

birthdays and annual anniversaries. Boyd couldn't stand any of us, but he needed us to make

things work. He started his business with 5 used cars. He paid cash for them, then kept buying

and selling, buying and selling."

She drains her wine glass and asks if he would mind refilling it. "The bottle is in the kitchen."

His stomach almost flips over when he sees how filthy the kitchen is. He returns to the living

room, bringing the wine bottle with him, and pours the wine into her glass. He can tell by the

way she smiles at him, that she likes him.

"Did Boyd pay you well Brenda?"

"No, he was very stingy. He hardly ever gave pay raises and as the company grew, he heaped

more responsibility on me. I finally told him I would quit if he didn't get me some help.

He thought it over for a few days, promoted me to accounts manager, and allowed me to hire 4 more women. He didn't hire men to work in the offices at that time because men would not take being screamed at and belittled. That was kind of his thing. Made him feel like a big man I guess.

Anyhow, the company kept growing. He was buying more and more cars. That is how he got so

rich. He did not fiancé the cars through banks or finance companies. He owned them outright. As

the responsibilities grew, I kept hiring more women. One day I met Ray when I drove over to the

Used Car division to question them about some questionable charges on the company credit card.

He was handsome and charming. I had worked there for years never knowing he worked there.

He was the manager of the Used Car Division. He explained that he had to wine and dine

potential companies and that he used the credit cards for that purpose. He claimed his father had

approved it. I knew he was lying, but he swept me off my feet. I buried his charges. We got

married at the courthouse with no family present. I had to go right back to work right after we

said I do.

Eventually, I started getting so many complaints about Ray and the Used Car Division. He was entertaining strippers in his office during working hours. He was taking his employees

out to drink at night and their wives and husbands were calling and complaining, not to mention

he did not know a thing about the car business. I hired another man, Charlie Bench to rescue the

used car business. He was Ray's assistant but he did all of the work."

"That must have been hard."

"Yes, it was. I got pregnant with Glenn on one of the rare nights he was home, and it was just me and Glenn most of the time. I had Ray followed by a private investigator when he didn't come

home for an entire month. I found out that Ray had a townhouse on the other side of town. He

would take all of his girlfriend's there."

"How did he pay for the townhouse without your knowledge?"

"He was selling cars and keeping the cash. I think he was selling drugs as well. I threatened to

leave Ray but he promised to use his Daddy's money to take Glenn away from me so, I stayed."

She pours another glass of wine.

"The funny thing is, Boyd never liked my son, Glenn. He somehow didn't believe he was Ray's.

So, he didn't have anything to do with me or him. He forbid Agnes to associate with Glenn. I ran

into Agnes at a shopping mall one day and she confided in me that Ray had told his father that

Glenn was not his child. I broke down right there in that mall, crying and screaming. I told her

that was not true. She hugged me and said, 'You know Brenda. Ray is all about the money. He

might not want to share the Boyd Motor money with his son if something ever happens to me

and Boyd.'

"I was devastated. How could Ray deny his own child? We lived separate lives after that happened. I confronted him. I bought this house and made him pay it off. I blackmailed him. I threatened to go to his Daddy and tell him Glenn really is his son. I threatened to tell Boyd about

his use of steroids, and how he was a fraud in the used car business. He paid off this house to keep me from telling the truth. The house is in my name, only. He gave me a new car every year after Glenn was born.

The money didn't come from Boyd Motors. I had access to the books and I knew where all the money was coming in and going to.

Almost four years ago, Boyd and Agnes were on a plane to go make offers on large dealerships

in Idaho and Oregon.

Boyd had the largest dealership in Washington but he wanted to take over the world. He was

drunk on power. It was on that trip that he had a massive heart attack. The airline returned them

to Washington and took him to the nearest hospital. Ray raced there to meet with him. He

brought Yammy Bleek, Boyd's attorney. Boyd thought he was dying and he gave Ray power of

attorney over the entire business. He turned everything over to him. Ray didn't even stay at the

hospital with his dad; he ran back here to the dealership and the first thing he did was fire me in

front of 25 employees. I told him to give me a few minutes to collect my things. I quickly

transferred (five hundred thousand dollars) to an account I had hidden from all of them. Then I

got my purse and walked out. It took him exactly 2 and a half years to destroy that business."

I am the one who went to the hospital and stayed with Agnes the entire time Boyd was in danger

of dying."

Detective Nugent reaches over pats her hand and says, "Brenda, I am truly sorry you went

through all of that. I am sure you did not deserve any of that abuse."

Brenda blushes and says, "Thanks for that sir. I don't feel like I did either. One of my previous employees, Karen Davis, would call me and keep me informed as to what was going on. She

finally quit when the pressure just got too much. She said she couldn't keep up with the money

that was disappearing from the accounts, and that Ray was on a massive spending spree of a

personal nature. She told me Ray was giving away cars, new and used to his drug buddies and

prostitutes. She also said, Ray had sold his parent's beautiful home in a quick sale, and put them in a rental. She said it was like watching a plane nose-dive."

"Does Ray give you money, Brenda?"

"Yes, he makes a lot of money selling Steroids and other drugs. He is so messed up that he

forgets he hates me sometimes and gives me money. I haven't had to dip into my retirement fund

yet."

Brenda laughs when she says that and Detective Nugent wants to arrest her right then, but he smiles.

"Why do you call it your retirement fund?" Detective Nugent asks.

"I earned that money, going for years with no raises, no promotions, putting up with Boyd and

Ray humiliating me in front of everyone. I will be able to retire and live comfortably off of that

well-deserved money."

Detective Nugent nods and smiles. Poor drunk, Brenda does not realize she has confessed to Felony Theft and Embezzlement to a police detective. He reaches over and pats her hand again and refills her wine.

In approximately 35 minutes Detective Plant gets the pictures he needs.

They leave and Detective Tope tells Brenda to stay in town in case they need her for more questioning. They step out on the porch. The wind is blowing hard, and they all are thankful for the clean air. They each breathe in deep to clear their lungs.

"Dear God, I need a shower, maybe 2. That house was awful. How does she live like that?" Detective Tope asks.

"The wine numbs her mind and her sense of smell." Detective Plant says and shakes his head.

Once in the car, Detective Tope tells Detective Nugent, "I think Miss Brenda is sweet on you

Nugent. She has cow eyes every time you walk in and she blushes like her demon child."

Nugent laughs and says, "I can't see being in a killer relationship like that." They both chuckle.

They return to the jail to speak to Glenn. He is angry. Word has reached him about his probation

being revoked and he will spend the entire 2 years in jail.

"I don't think I have anything to say to you assholes today because I feel like you are behind my probation being voked."

Detective Nugent says, "RE-VOKED. You are saying it wrong."

"Whatever!" screams Glenn.

"We just want to talk to you about your Mama."

Glenn looks suspicious and says, "What about Brenda?"

"What is your relationship with her?"

"There ain't no relationship. She treats me like crap. She kind of cut me off."

"What do you mean?

"She's screwed up in the head. She kicked my old man out of the house. All she does is sit in

front of the TV. watching cop shows all day and night, drinking her wine. She used to bring me food that she cooked all of the time, then she stopped one day, just stopped, no explanation. It

was wrong as far as I was concerned."

"How did you and your grandparents eat?"

"I would go out and get us something, or my old man would bring us food," Glenn says, as his

eyes shift to the right, not making eye contact.

"Did the Wrights eat every day?" Detective Tope asks.

"Yeah of course," Glenn says, looking away.

The detectives' glance at each other, knowing full well the coroner stated the Wrights were emaciated.

"Where did you get money to buy food to feed your grandparents?"

"My old man gave it to me."

"Where did he get the money?"

"Um, he works at some gym."

"Listen Glenn. He told us that he only works 3 or maybe 4 days a week. There is no way he can

rent a house for the Wrights, help keep up your mom, and feed everybody on a little job like that.

"Where is the money coming from?"

"Oh yeah. They get something called social security money."

"Do you take them to get the checks cashed?"

"No, they don't like to go out. I guess Ray is over their checks. He cashes them and either gives

me the money to feed them or he brings the food. Can I go now? I'm not feeling so hot

today."

"Yeah." The detectives say as they stand up and knock on the door to be let out of the interview

room.

Detective Plant meets them back at their office. "Hello, guys. I will have these pictures ready for

you tomorrow afternoon. I think I found something that might interest both of you.

Everyone goes home for the day, leaving the night shift to solve their own cases.

Neither Tope nor Nugent sleeps well. Their brains won't shut off. They keep thinking they are

missing something.

The next morning, they search Ray's residence. It is only the garage of a friend, Mason Thread.

There is only a couch, a fan, a television, Ray's clothing, some dirty magazines, and a

refrigerator filled with salad fixings and Gatorade. There is no paperwork there.

They do find a strong box that is filled with credit cards that have Boyd and Agnes Wright's names on them. The detectives collect them and take them to the Financial Crimes Division, Detective Rivera, so she can investigate.

As soon as they are back in the office, the telephone rings, it is Brenda, and she is drunk.

"I just remembered something important. There is a safety deposit box with burial policies in it at First National Daily Bank. Boyd put me on the account as being one of the people who can access the safety deposit box. It's only Agnes, him, and me." She hiccups.

Detective Nugent asks, "What kind of policies are in the box, Brenda?"

"I know there are Burial policies but I don't know what else. They were put in there over 20

years ago. Maybe a headstone policy? I don't know."

"Okay, we will pick you up in the morning and we will take you to the band. Please do not drink anymore tonight. Drink some coffee in the morning and DO NOT tell anyone about this safety

deposit box."

"I won't I promise, but can you come over?." Brenda says as she begins to cry.

"We will be there at 9 am. Go take a hot shower and get some sleep."

Brenda whispers, "Okay", and Detective Nugent hangs up.

Tope smiles and says, "I think she is trying to seduce you."

Nugent rolls his eyes and says, "Ewww."

As promised, they pick Brenda up at 9 am. She is hungover. They go to the bank manager, who escorts them to the safety deposit room. There is a large table in the room. Brenda and the manager insert their keys and open the box. They lay out all of the policies and letters. Not only are there life insurances for Boyd and Agnes. The executive is Brenda Wright. The life insurances total 3 million dollars. There is a note attached stating, "Brenda we are so sorry we didn't believe Glenn was our grandson. Please accept this money as our apology. Do not share with Ray. He doesn't deserve you or any more of our money."

Attached to the Burial policy, there is a receipt, paid in full, for 2 burial plots at Newport Acres, a local cemetery owned by Robertson Funeral Home. There are receipts of the headstones having been paid for in full and, a receipt showing the flowers have been paid for in full. A note attached to all of this states, "The burial policy will cover the Robertson Funeral Home's expenses (the casket and the funeral). I want to be buried in a blue suit, blue shirt, and dark blue tie; Agnes wants to be buried in a white dress. Thank you for honoring our wishes."

Brenda breaks down and cries.

Detective Tope says, "Brenda, you cannot take the life insurance policies yet, because we are still investigating the murders."

Detective Nugent says, "But you can take the other policies to the funeral home to show what is paid for to get the funeral started. We will take you there now."

He gave her his handkerchief. Brenda nodded that she understood.

When they arrived at Robertson's Funeral Home the young man, Mr. Tyler was very nice and took all the paperwork from them and wrote down Brenda's contact information.

The detectives took Brenda back to her residence. On the ride home, she says, "I had no earthly

idea they left me any life insurance policies. So many years ago, we only put the burial policies

in that safety deposit box. Ray did not know about that box or he would have demanded his

name be put on the access page."

Detective Nugent believed her, but Tope did not. He called the bank manager and asked when

was the last time anyone had signed to have entry or access to that safety deposit box. She put

him on hold while she checked. In a few minutes she came back and said, Mrs. Agnes Wright

had entered 17 years ago. That is the last time anyone was in the safety deposit box until today."

"Did Brenda Wright ever sign into the safety deposit box without the Wrights?"

"No sir. Only when they first rented the box."

"How did it remain open? Who paid for it to stay open?"

"Boyd Wright paid in advance for 50 years."

When he got off the telephone, he looked at Nugent and said, "Your girl is telling the truth. No

one has been in that safety deposit box in 17 years until today."

The telephone rings, it is the coroner.

"What's up? Sammie." Detective Nugent says.

"Hey Nugent. Listen, Robertson Funeral Home just called and wants to know when they can

pick up the bodies for cremation."

Nugent stands up and yells, "What the hell?"

The coroner says, "Yep, that's what he said."

"Do NOT release the bodies to him until we get over there and speak to him. There are burial

policies bought and paid for by the victims for a real funeral. I will call you from the funeral

home. Thanks, Sammie."

The detective slams the telephone down and barks, "Come on Tope, we have some ass to kick."

Detective Tope drives to the Funeral Home because he recognizes Detective Nugent is too angry

to be behind the wheel of a car.

Mr. Tyler looks terrified when he looks up and sees them stomping through his lobby.

"I need to speak with you now!" Detective Nugent yells.

Mr. Tyler excuses himself from the family he is currently speaking with about their family's

funeral arrangements.

"Please step into my office gentlemen." Mr. Tyler asks. His voice is nearly trembling.

"Cut the crap Tyler. I just received a call from the coroner. What is this about cremating the

Wrights?" Detective Nugent yells.

It's, it's what the family wants." Tyler stutters.

Detective Tope picks up Tyler's office telephone, without asking, and dials Brenda's number. She

answers on the first ring.

"Brenda, have you lost your mind?"

"No sir! Mr. Tyler convinced me that the funeral home would be losing money since the policy

was taken out so long ago, and he said, I would be responsible for paying the extra money they

would be losing. He said it will be easier and quicker to just do the cremations. He is insisting

that I go ahead with the cremations."

Tope handed Detective Nugent the telephone. "Brenda, it's Detective Nugent. Listen, the Wrights WILL get the burial they wanted and paid for. I will handle Mr. Tyler."

Brenda starts to cry. "Listen, Brenda, you did not do anything wrong. You need to calm down. I

will call you back in a few minutes." And he hangs up.

Nugent turns to a pale-looking Tyler and says, "I will charge you with fraud you son of a bitch.

Mr. and Mrs. Boyd Wright will get the funeral they paid for, the plots they paid for, and the

flowers they paid for; they will also get the headstones your father sold them. Do you understand

me? I swear by everything that is holy and legal. I will have this business shut down by our local

and state government if you mess up this funeral, or if you don't do right by these victims. There

will be some very important visitors in attendance for the funeral. Media… and lots of it,

Newspaper reporters, News reports, and Press of every kind. I am expecting at least 24 press

personnel here. If you screw up one thing, I will personally give an interview and point out your shortcomings. If you don't believe me, TRY ME!

Mr. Tyler apologized profusely. "It will be a lovely service, I promise. I will go now and collect the bodies."

"There is one more thing. The Wright's little dog Angus has passed away. We want him buried in

his own little baby casket. He will be buried between Mr. and Mrs. Boyd. He was very special to

them. You will not charge Brenda Wright one solitary cent for this funeral. It has all been paid for

in the policies we brought you this afternoon. Are we clear?"

Tyler swallows hard and says, "Yes, sir. I understand." He leaves quickly, nearly running.

Detective Tope laughs and says, "You look like a family member of Brenda's, you are red in the

face." Nugent just shakes his head. And says, "damn crooks are everywhere."

He calls the coroner, "Sammie, I got that idiot funeral director straightened out so it is okay to release the bodies, including the dog to Robertson Funeral Home. You are invited to the funeral if you have time. Thanks for everything man."

Brenda calls right back. "I, I don't have a blue suit for Boyd or a white dress for Agnes."

Detective Nugent is still annoyed so he says, "Brenda, I can think of 500,000 reasons you can afford to buy those things for them."

Brenda hesitates then says, "I, uh, I told you about that?"

Nugent laughs and says, "Yes you did dear. But it's our little secret."

Brenda is quiet for a second then says, "I don't know what size to buy."

Nugent says, "The funeral home will measure them, then let you know. It will be okay."

Detective Tope is about to bust a gut. He wants to laugh so bad.

Nugent says, " I will speak to you later, get some rest." And hangs up. He rolls his eyes and shakes his head. "Damn Tope, I've had girlfriends I didn't talk to as much as I do this one."

Tope laughs, "I think she is growing on you."

"Shut up."

Brenda calls them back at their office. Mr. Tyler has called her and apologized and gave her the

sizes of the suit and the dress. Brenda went shopping, purchased the items, and delivered them to

the funeral home.

The next morning, Mr. Tyler is so nervous he is about to pee his pants. Detective Nugent is there

to make sure everything is going according to plan. Nugent gave Mr. Tyler a list of all the Media

that would be in attendance. There were 24 names on the list. Nugent had stayed up all night

long calling in favors all over the state. He knew there would be much more than 24. He wants

the element of surprise to scare Mr. Tyler. Nugent also wants Tyler to know he is delivering on

his promise to ruin him, if he messes up this funeral.

A blanket statement has been given to all media productions. There were flowers and plants from

each of the media companies. The sprays of flowers on Boyd and Agnes coffins were stunning.

The funeral home provides a limousine for Brenda. She requests Detectives Nugent and Tope

ride with her since she had no family. Detective Plant and Lieutenant Haney rode together in a

Patrol vehicle.

This is the statement that all media is reporting to the public.

"Mr. and Mrs. Boyd Wright, an elderly husband and wife, formerly mega-millionaires, owned the largest Ford dealership in the entire state of Washington, was brutally murdered on August 15, 1985. The case is still currently under investigation. The Wright's Son, Ray and their grandson, Glenn have been arrested and are being held in the Spanish

County Jail on unrelated charges. A tiny coffin holds the Wright's dog, Angus, who has passed away. He will be buried between the Wright's who loved him dearly. Robertson's Funeral Home was chosen by Boyd and Agnes Wright years ago to be the handlers of their final resting place. The funeral home graciously donated the baby coffin for the Wright's dog, and his name will be etched on their headstone."

Mr. Tyler was secretly fuming. His father had sold those things to Boyd Wright 22 years ago,

back when the prices were cheap. This funeral was costing him a small fortune. However, the

detectives had him by the short hairs and he knew it. All he could do was honor the policies and

pray there were no more out there. On the other hand, maybe all the press would increase his

business.

Ray Wright was furious that he was not allowed to go to his parent's funeral. He threw his food

tray at a guard, fought with another inmate, and was put into solitary confinement. He was not

even allowed to watch it on television, as he posed a threat to himself and others.

The Warden stated, "It is just too big of a risk to take Ray to the funeral and he goes crazy and

hurt someone there."

Glenn Wright is informed of the funeral, but did not care. He did not want to go. He showed no emotion nor interest.

Brenda has a King-size hangover and she reeks of wine. She is dressed in black from head to toe.

Detective Nugent stands behind her, squeezes her hand, and whispers, "You picked out a very

nice suit for Boyd, and Agnes' dress is very sweet. You look very nice too. You did good hon"

Brenda smiles, blushes and says, "Thanks."

There is a huge turnout. Mainly the press and police are in attendance. A chaplain associated

with the funeral home officiates the funeral. Detective Nugent had lied to Mr. Tyler, there were

not 24, there were over 50 reporters and representatives of the media. The police Chief sent his

Media representative to give a small statement on behalf of the department.

"Hello. I am Captain Jake Owens. Media Representative for Spanish Trail Police Department. The murder of Boyd and Agnes Wright is still under investigation. We will make a full statement as soon as this case has been solved. Our officers are working hard to find who is responsible for this horrible crime. Thank you for being here to honor this family." With that, he poses for a few fast pictures and steps away from the podium.

Detectives Tope and Nugent try not to smile. Captain Owens is a media whore. He loves to see his face on television, in newspapers, and in crime magazines. They admit he is handsome, a pretty boy. They just thank God they don't have to work with him. His ego is too large for his head to come thru their office doors.

Detectives Nugent and Tope feel a sense of relief when the funeral is over. They hope the Wrights are finally at peace. They deserve to be at peace with their little dog.

The limosine takes them back to the funeral home. The detectives don't wait to see Mr. Tyler, they leave in their car. Both are aggravated.

"3 dead bodies, nothing but circumstantial evidence on the 2 family members in custody. This is driving me crazy. We don't have enough to charge them with murder, just abuse. " Detective Nugent says.

"Is there something we are missing in that house?" Tope asks.

"Let's stop in again and recheck it."

The detectives drive back to the Wright's neighborhood.

As they pulled into the driveway, they noticed another vehicle was there. They slowly

approached the front door and a lady comes out, carrying a notepad and pen.

"Hello. I'm Vivian Le'braun. I am the real estate agent in charge of this house. I don't know how

I will ever rent or even sell it after this."

Detective Nugent finds it hard to feel sorry for her. "You will forgive me if my sympathy lies

with the murder victims. We just came from their funerals." He said sourly.

She looks stunned but regroups and says, "Why yes, of course, I didn't mean to sound callous.

I'm glad you came now because the owner of the house has had the locks changed to try and

keep vagrants out of here. Here is a key for you. I was going to bring it by your office later

today."

Detective Tope speaks up. "Well, this is convenient. Listen, are you aware of any hidden

passages, or hidden spaces or just anywhere things could be hidden in this house Did we miss

something in our search?"

Vivian thought for a moment and said, "Did you check the attic?"

They both say, "Attic?". They had not seen an attic door.

"It's been wallpapered over, to disguise it. The owner did it years ago. An incident happened

where his daughters went missing and they were hiding in the attic. They fell asleep and were

missing for 4 hours. He closed it up after they found the girls. Follow me please," Vivian says.

She leads them to an attic opening, covered by painted wood, the same color as the wall. It has a

small string painted over and attached to the wall.

"I don't remember seeing this Tope, do you?"

"No, I don't remember it either."

"You wouldn't have, like I said before, it's camouflaged on purpose," Vivian says.

When they pull the string from the wall, the attic ladder comes down. Both Detective Nugent and

Detective Tope say, "Stay here Vivian." at the same time.

There are hundreds of VHR tapes in the attic. A camera is pointed directly at the Wright's

bedroom, the bathroom, the living room, the hall, the kitchen, and the empty dining room.

"It's going to take us a long time to check all of these tapes," Tope said.

"Well, we will just have to recruit some help."

They go back downstairs to Vivian. Detective Nugent goes outside to use his radio and contact

his Lieutenant. The Lieutenant has the crime scene team come and retrieve all of the tapes and

transport them to the training room. Then he calls the Chief of Police and asks permission to

bring some guys in for overtime to view the tapes. He agreed.

In 3 hours, they recruit 8 officers who are officially off duty. The training room has 10 VCR

players and televisions. They each are given notepads, pens, drinks, and pizza. Their job is to document what is on each tape. Plus, they are making $20.00 an hour to help view the tapes.

The majority of the tapes are of Agnes and Boyd wandering around their bedroom trying to get out of a locked door. There are tapes of them looking into an empty refrigerator and empty

kitchen cabinets. It is starting to look like typical sad stuff. Finally, one of the officers says, "I

think you need to see this, guys."

They walk over to him. A man in a black mask was whipping Agnes with a belt. She was begging him to stop. He made her lay across the bed and he continues to whip her.

The assailant was not Ray. He was bigger and had no tattoos. Boyd tries to stop him. The man throws Boyd against the wall and continues hitting Agnes with the belt. Boyd slid down the wall

and did not move. Someone comes in. The masked guy started jumping up and down, euphoric.

"Whoo that was a rush man. How much do I owe you?"

"What's it worth to you?" the muffled voice asked.

"Here's $80.00. I will pay $100 next time."

The tape ends. Detective Nugent said, "This case is kicking my butt. Let's keep going."

Another officer calls out, "I need you guys."

In this video, Ray is chasing Boyd outside. All Boyd had on was his boxer shorts. He was shivering. There is snow on the ground. Ray grabs him by his neck and marches him back inside, slapping the back of his head repeatedly, with every step. Boyd was crying. Ray is putting cigarettes out on his father.

"I got one you need to see, Detectives. "Another officer calls out. This video shows Agnes and Boyd being given a box of chicken and Glenn is screaming like a maniac, "Hurry up eat up, I have to go, Hurry up!" They were eating as fast as they could. Agnes starts to choke and Glenn grabs her face and screams, "If you puke you will regret it." Boyd tries to slip a few pieces of chicken to his dog and Glenn catches him. He tackles Boyd and drags him to his room, then he opens the front door and kicks the little dog like a football. Agnes faints. He drags her to the bedroom and body slams her on the floor hard.

Another video shows Ray and Glenn eating a huge meal. They are throwing a few scraps to Boyd and Agnes like they are dogs. It was heart-wrenching.

The officers are so disgusted. They somehow managed to watch every video. One shows Agnes being sexually assaulted by 2 men who had shirts covering their faces. They pay Glenn $100 cash for the experience. He is very cordial. "Come back any time. We are always open." He says with a hearty laugh.

There is a video of Agnes tied up and Glenn and Ray putting Glenn's House Arrest Monitor on

her ankle.

Another video showed Ray blowing crack smoke in their faces then burning Boyd with

cigarettes and laughing hysterically. Boyd runs into the kitchen with Glenn and Ray following

him. Glenn knocks him down, sits on his back, and starts punching him in the chest. Ray pulls

Glenn off. His father rolls over, and Ray stabs his father in the back, underneath the shoulder

blade, into his heart from behind. Killing him.

Detective Nugent tells Detective Tope, "Thank God they are dead. They suffered so much."

He tears up. "I wish I could have 10 minutes alone with Ray and Glenn. They did this for what? Revenge? Ray didn't feel loved or appreciated, and Glenn sold them for crack."

The Chief of Police and their Lieutenant come down to the training room to view some of the tapes.

"Holy Crap, you guys look bad. Were the tapes enough evidence? Have we got them?"

Detective Nugent didn't trust himself to speak, so Detective Tope said, "Yes, sir. We have enough

on Ray and Glenn Wright to charge them both with Felony first-degree Murder of Boyd Wright.

Chief, please if you have any pull in the DA's office, please ask them not to make a plea deal.

Ray and Glenn deserve to go to the gas chamber for this. These were decent, hardworking

people, who were tortured for almost a year, then murdered."

The Chief said, "I will head over there right now. For what it's worth Detectives Nugent and Tope you did a great job solving this case."

As the chief walks out the door, one last officer says, "I think you are going to want to see this last one sir."

Detective Tope walks over and sees Brenda on the screen. She is screaming at Agnes then hits

her over the head with a large piece of pottery. Then she grabs a jagged piece of the pottery and

sticks it in Agnes' neck, killing her instantly.

"Well, I'll be damned. Nugent, you ain't gonna believe this."

Detective Nugent walks over and is stunned.

They run out of the building to their car. They call dispatch and ask them to please have a patrol

unit meet them at Brenda's house. She is just backing out of her driveway when the patrol car

blocks her in. The patrol officer removes her from her car, handcuff her, and puts her in the back

of the patrol car.

Detective Nugent is still stunned. She has fooled him. Not many criminals has that ability but she did. She seems so much like a victim herself.

They squeal their tires as they turn on Brenda's Street. She is smiling as Detective Nugent pulls her out of the patrol car.

"Okay copper, you got me." Brenda says with a smile.

"I just want to know why Brenda?"

Detective Tope gets back in their car and waits for Detective Nugent to handle this. He is emotionally spent. This day has been exhausting.

Brenda bites her lip, then speaks... "I took them some food over there, that is when Ray tells me that Boyd is going to turn Glenn in to the police. As bad as he is, he is still my kid. Agnes starts talking gibberish, it's like she forgot how to speak English or something. I was mad. I told her and Boyd they better not turn Glenn in to the police. Boyd starts trying to talk and him and Glenn get into a pushing match. Glenn and Ray rough him up. I went into the kitchen to tell them to stop, but Boyd was already dead. Agnes was standing in the hallway crying. I was going to walk past her but she reached out and she touched my arm, she didn't even grab me or hit me, she just touched my arm. I flipped out. There was a planter on the porch with a dead plant in it. I went and picked it up and hit her over the head with it. It stunned her. The way she looked at me, almost like I disappointed her. I picked up a broken piece of the pottery and stuck it in her neck. It was over for both of us, over for all of us because I knew Ray and Glenn had killed Boyd a few minutes before that. How did you find out?"

"Glenn had cameras installed all over the house in the attic. We have it on tape."

She smiles and says, "You got me. What is it you guys say? Don't do the crime if you can't do the time?"

"I'm just curious. Why did you quit taking food over there?"

"I caught Glenn trading the food for crack. So I stopped."

Detective Nugent is physically ill after seeing all of those videos, and then to see that Brenda is involved is just so unexpected.

He says, "Brenda, you are going to need a good lawyer and they cost money. Where did you hide that money, you took? I can have a good lawyer get in touch with you.

A good lawyer can work magic for you. You are too good a person to go to prison. I know you are good; you have a good heart. Maybe you are just what I need. Maybe we can help each other."

Brenda looks shocked. "You will do that for me?"

He lightly touched her cheek with his hand, "Yes I will. And when the attorney gets you out of

this mess, you can cash in those 2 life insurance policies. You will be free."

Her eyes light up, then she smiles and says, "The money is here at Westside Community Bank. It's under my mother's name, Shirley Pemberton. She's been dead for years. I just kept the account open and used it when I needed it. I put my face on her ID and they never questioned my using the account."

He smiles at her and says "Brenda, I hope you are fed with the same spoon you fed the Wrights with." And shuts the door.

Detective Nugent tells the patrolman that they will meet him at the jail. When he walks back to the car., Tope asks, "What was that about? It looked like a tender moment from here."

"She confessed to everything, then the stupid idiot told me where the stolen money is. I think she might have been under the assumption that I was going to help her get a great attorney with all that money. Boy was she wrong."

When they got back to the office, Detective Plant had some more pictures for them. The knife

that was in Boyd's back was a match for knives found in Brenda's kitchen. There was blood-

stained men's and women's clothing also found in the bottom of the 2nd garbage bag.

The Financial Crimes Division filed charges against Brenda for Embezzlement and Fraud. She

was also charged with Murder One.

Brenda, Ray, and Glenn all received the death penalty after their trials. Those punishments were

later commuted to life in prison without the possibility of parole, when the State of Washington

abolished the death penalty.

Ray was killed in prison after 7 years. Glenn committed suicide after 5 years. Brenda is still

serving her sentence at Ranbury Women's Maximum Correctional Facility. She teaches

accounting courses and works as a secretary in the library. Financial Crimes was able to retrieve

the stolen five hundred thousand dollars and it was put into Washington State funding for victims

of violent crimes; since there were no surviving relatives. The life insurance policies were

deemed invalid due to murder and the executor being the murderer.

This story is fiction. It is set in the year 1985 when Washington still had the death penalty. That changed in the late 1980's. They abolished the death penalty and changed it life in prison.

However, the FBI, Police Officers, Deputy Sheriffs, Marshals, Correctional Officers, and all other law enforcement officers see things every day that damage them. They may smile and take it on the chin, but it leaves a mark on their heart and in their minds. Some people pretend to be callous, and hard but I have seen the largest men cry over molested children and murdered citizens. They didn't have the cameras in police cars and the microphones on their tie clips back in the 1980s. In every profession, there are good and bad workers.

I honestly believe there should be a 5-year limit on the amount of time people can be patrol officers. Statistics prove that Law enforcement officers have

- The highest suicide rates
- The highest divorce rates
- The highest alcoholism rates

No logical person could see so much death and destruction and not be affected by what they see. I found out many years after I ended my Law enforcement career that I have PTSD. I still have nightmares of me being a cop, pulling my gun, and it falls apart in my hand. Also, I have dreams of being shot. I feel myself take my last breath, I hear the air going out of my lungs and I wake up in terror, gasping for air. There are other night terrors I suffer from, but I won't bore you with my problems, I just wanted you to know that officers are affected by their jobs. You may see them as the bad guys but they are the heroes in many stories. I can't tell you how many times we rescued men, women, and children from so many dangerous situations. Nobody ever said thank you. We just handled the call and went on to the next place that the dispatcher sent us.

I worked with some bad cops. I remember going into a house where we knew the guy was armed and dangerous. A male officer pulled me in front of him, like a shield. I was so stunned. I never told a soul because there is a code, if you break the code, you are in the wrong, no matter what. They freeze you out, you can't be trusted if you tell on one of your own.

Another time, I requested back up. The officer was suppose to help me search the house to look for the suspect. He didn't help me.

I found the bad guy hiding in a closet under a bunch of clothes. I called to the other officer to come in and assist me. I covered (pointed my gun at the suspect to make sure the officer was safe) while he handcuffed the guy and walked him out to the patrol car. Other officers had arrived and this guy looked like a hero. I said nothing to contradict his 15 minutes of fame. Later I pulled his report and he had written that I did nothing to assist him in the arrest.

I also worked with some great officers. Those officers worked with me as a team. They came running when I called for backup. They treated me as their equal and showed me great respect.

I admired them and the valor they used in their professions. They were proud to protect our city and county.

I am attaching various incidents that may or may not have happened during the 10 and a half years of my law enforcement career. That section is Unit 29. It was my patrol car number. When the dispatch called me, they called, "Dispatch to unit 29..."

Unit 29

By Lilly Buchanan

74

All characters are fictional, and the
stories are in no way true in any form
except in the author's imagination.

Officer 29

1990

Lilly Buchanan, Author

Dedication

This selection of stories is dedicated to all officers far and wide. May you be safe, and seek the professional help you so desperately deserve by the time your shift is done. Beneke you rock!

Officer Elizabeth Tilly, Unit 29, is on patrol, day shift. It is 102 degrees outside. There are 3 lanes of traffic stopped at the red lights. The far-left lane is a turn lane. It turned green. Unfortunately, the vehicle to the patrol car's right went straight through the red light. It seems like every citizen in all of America turned toward Tilly to ensure she saw the car run the red light. Tilly makes the stop.

Tilly bumps her siren, flashes her blue light, and pulls the car over.

"Ma'am, obviously you ran the red light while you were next to a police car. I am sure it was not on purpose. I'm just going to run your license with our dispatcher if you are clear, I will let you go with a warning."

"Oh, my god. I am so sorry. The nursery called and said something is wrong with my child. I just ran out of the house and jumped in my car and started driving to the nursery. I don't have my license with me. "

"It's okay, just give me your name and birth date. They can run it by that."

"Alicia Mctree, O9091982."

Tilly calls in her name and in a matter of minutes the dispatcher calls on the radio.

"Tilly that has a 7400 (warrant) for DUI and Battery."

"That's 10-4 dispatch. Send my Sergeant and a 1015 (tow truck)"

Tilly says, "Ma'am I'm going to ask you to please step out of your car. You have a warrant for your arrest."

"Wait! Please. I gave you my sister's information. I will give you my real name and birthdate."

It is now 103 degrees outside and Tilly is heated inside and out.

Tilly opens the door of her car and the female slams it shut. She is attempting to drive off.

Tilly opens the car door wide before the driver can shut it and seizes the driver.

"Ma'am please don't make this worse than it has to be! Just cooperate."

The woman looks defeated and gets out of the car on her own. Tilly puts her in the back of her patrol car. Tilly states...

"Ma'am you are under arrest for giving false information to a law enforcement officer. You have the right to remain silent. Everything you say can and will be used against you in a court of law. You have the right to an attorney. If you cannot afford one, one will be appointed to you." Tilly closes the door.

Inside Tilly's car feels cold from the air conditioning. She notices the lady in the backseat is sweating, yet Tilly is not. She thinks that odd but continues filling out her arrest paperwork.

"Care to share your real information with me?" meeting the woman's eyes in the rearview mirror.

"I'm Rachel Brenda Vegas. My birthday is May 12, 1987."

Tilly calls in the woman's real name, there is a warrant for her arrest. Tilly tells the woman about the warrant.

"I know." She says with her head down. She is crying.

Sergeant Hayes arrives, and together they inventory Rachel's vehicle. Tilly asked the woman, "Ma'am do you want your purse?"

The woman hesitates and says, "No, I'm fine."

This is a huge red flag for Officer Tilly, what woman doesn't want her purse?

In the large purse, Tilly finds 225 small bags of crack cocaine, individually ready for distribution. Under the front passenger seat is a Smith and Wesson 45 caliber and a butcher knife. The Sergeant tests the drugs and verifies it is Crack Cocaine. They bag the drugs and seal them. Both Tilly and Sergeant Hayes sign their names on the bag as having the drugs in their custody. This practice is for the evidence room. It's called chain of custody.

"You take her to jail and I will take the drugs and weapons to headquarters. Don't forget to add the charges of the weapons when you do the drug charge and don't forget to make it with intent to distribute. Forward a copy to Metro Narcotics. They will need this information." The sergeant reminds Tilly.

Tilly nods her head yes. She knows how to do this but the Sergeant is always very detail oriented. He is a helicopter Sergeant, always hovering over his staff. If they mess up, he takes it personally. He has trained them better.

Once the tow truck leaves, Tilly gets back in her car. While she drinks a few sips of water she tells the lady about the new charges. The female begins to scream and cry. She is rocking back and forth shaking the patrol car. She starts to beg Tilly.

"Please do not let my kids go to Aunt Freda. Please oh god please don't. Please promise me you will protect them. If she gets her hands on them...oh promise me, please!"

Tilly assures her that she will get DCFS (Department of Children and Family Services) involved and tell them what she is saying.

Tilly radios dispatch, "Dispatch this is unit 29 I am en route to the county jail with one white female"

Dispatch advises Tilly to stay in her location. "That is negative unit 29. Stay in your location."

Before Tilly can question, 2 black Yukon's appear in front of and in back of Tilly's patrol car and block her vehicle in. The occupants, men dressed in black suits, jump out and start to remove the prisoner from the back of the patrol car. Tilly jumps out, gun drawn and screams, "What the fuck? Who are you?"

One of them quickly flashes a badge. "FBI special agents. I'm officer Nunya and he is officer Damn and the driver is officer Business. Now stand down or I will shoot you in your motherfucking head and tell the world she did it." nodding towards the prisoner.

The prisoner is hysterical. They take the handcuffs off of her and throw them in the street, shoving the prisoner in the back of their car.

Tilly can still hear her screaming, "Don't forget my kids! You promised!" Tilly then heard a loud punch or thud, then silence. They immediately speed away.

Tilly starts to feel "off" like she might faint. She keys up the microphone to call dispatch but she is in shock, not having the words to speak.

By keying up her radio dispatch knows she is trying to make contact.

"That's 10-4. You are en route to headquarters."

Tilly starts to panic. She knew she didn't say that. Her mouth is dry and her tongue feels swollen. She is not sweating and her heart is pounding.

Her cellphone rings and it is her Sergeant.

"I feel like something is wrong... with me. I am sick. My prisoner is gone."

"I know I can explain it. Everything is okay, can you make it to the jail? Just meet me at the Jail. If you have any water, drink it."

Tilly could not open the cooler on her passenger seat floor, her hands seemed not to work. She could hear the Sergeant's voice.

"Dispatch, this Sergeant Hayes. Unit 29 is going to meet me at the jail. Please have a nurse on standby. This is code 3. (Code 3 medical emergency)

Tilly does not remember walking into the jail. However, she did walk into the Jail on her own. She shakes the intake officer's hand, then faints on the floor.

Tilly wakes up at the hospital. They had given her 3 bags of intravenous fluids and used ice bags and towels to help her cool down.

When she is fully awake, she sees her entire police squad in her room, including her Sergeant and the Captain. It startles her.

"Where am I? What happened?"

The captain speaks up, "You are going to be okay Tilly. You had a heat stroke. However, I am going to have to write you up for being out of uniform."

He looks down at her chest. Tilly also looks down and her entire uniform shirt is wide open with her black lacy bra completely exposed. She grabs her shirt to close it and pulls the sheet up. They all laugh as she turns red as a traffic light.

Yelling at her squad, "You goofs probably bribed the nurse to leave it open."

"I got $10.00 says she is wearing matching panties." Called out Officer Williams, waving his $10.00 bill. They laugh again.

A nurse enters the room and purrs, "Gosh you are so lucky to work with all these handsome men."

Tilly snorts, "You wouldn't think so if you heard them burping and farting all the time. I'm not even going to mention the scratching of the balls or arranging their swords."

Officer Swain speaks up, "Hey we are proud of our swords."

Tilly whispers, "Swain, I've heard about your sword. You shouldn't be proud."

Again, laughter fills the room.

The doctor comes in and clears Tilly to be released to go home and put on bed rest for 3 days.

"Officer Tilly. You are not supposed to have all these visitors, however, since they are all carrying firearms, I'm going to let it slide this time. You need to stay on bed rest for a couple of days until you can get your strength back. Stay out of the heat. Heat strokes take a lot out of you. Drink plenty of fluids, water, and electrolyte fluids like Gatorade or Powerade."

Sergeant Hayes drives Tilly home and Officer Masey drives her patrol car to her home. The Sergeant assures Tilly everything was okay and she just needed to rest.

Once Tilly gets home, she remembers the little girls. She calls DCFS and tells them about the prisoner and her children. She explains there is no report yet, due to her illness, but since she knows the case manager personally and she agrees to meet them at the address given by the arrested female.

Tilly defies doctors' orders and meets DCFS agent Monique Fetty at the address given. It is a crack house. Tilly calls her Sergeant on the telephone and he meets her there with 3 squad cars.

"Damn it, Tilly, you are in so much trouble! You are supposed to be on home rest! For Christ's sake, I just took you home from the hospital!" the Sergeant tries not to scream but his voice is raised and that vein is standing up on the side of his head.

"I'm sorry Sergeant. I just remembered the prisoner had 3 little girls that she was scared for and I had to meet DCFS out here to be sure they were okay."

"Fine, stay out here, as a matter of a fact, get in my damn car!" the Sergeant growls.

The patrols go into the house and the occupants scatter like roaches. There are 3 dead bodies inside. The officers capture 6 people and arrest them for possession of drugs and fleeing arrest. There are no children inside.

The Sergeant starts toward Tilly and says, "Pain in my ass you are girl! 3 DOAs inside. All overdoses. I called for the coroner."

A talk with the neighbors helps Sergeant Hayes, DCFS and Officer Tilly discover there are 3 girls belonging to Rachel Vegas at another neighbor's house 3 doors down.

They walk over to the house and knock on the door. A woman answers cautiously, peeking thru a crack in the door.

"What do you want? I didn't call the police to my house."

"Ma'am we are doing a welfare check on Rachel Vega's 3 daughters. Are they here with you?"

"Why yes, they are and you can tell that bitch that she owes me some money. She was supposed to pick them up yesterday."

Tilly digs in her pocket and pulls out $60.00 and gives it to the woman.

"We need to speak to the children."

"Thanks for the money but now is not a good time. They sleeping."

The woman starts to close the door but Tilly pushes in before anyone can stop her and begins to call the kids. The entire house is clear except for one locked door.

Sergeant Hayes asks the woman to open the door but she smirks and turns her head as if she didn't hear him. He kicks the door in and there are the 3 girls laying on a filthy mattress, with no sheet. They are passed out cold. On the floor are 4 large, empty Nyquil bottles. They have been drugged to make them sleep. All three girls have bruises on their arms and bloody marks on their legs from tree switches. A large switch lies on the floor. The woman tries to run but is detained by officers outside. An ambulance is called to take the children to the hospital to make sure they are okay. Officer Michaels is still carrying the wig he pulled off of the woman's head when trying to apprehend her. The Sergeant shakes his head and tells the Rookie to give it back to the woman. In spite, the rookie put it back on her head backward. It looked ridiculous.

Officer Tilly goes home to finally get her rest. She sleeps fitful and feels worse the next day. There is nothing to watch on the four hundred channels of cable she pays for and no food in her kitchen. She orders a pizza. In one hour when the doorbell rings, she opens the door with cash in hand to see her squad eating her pizza.

"We saved you one piece. Can't have you getting fat, now, can we?"

"What in the hell? Guys, one piece really?"

"Quit your bitching and get dressed, be downstairs in 5 minutes. We will whisk you thru a drive-thru. Someone checked all 3 girls out of the hospital against medical advice. We've got an address."

Tilly called the case manager, and she and her supervisor agreed to meet them at the address.

Once in the patrol car, Tilly asked the Corporal,

"Dane, do you have any idea what happened yesterday with my prisoner?"

"Well, we have been warned not to talk about it, the Chief and those guys will brief you when it's time. It was legitimate in a twisted sort of way. I'm glad you didn't get hurt. Those guys can be real pricks."

Tilly and Dane pulled up at a well-maintained house in middle-class suburbia. It even had a white picket fence and a porch swing.

The other patrol cars showed up at about the same time. They approached the house and saw a woman waving her dishcloth at them.

"Y'all come on it. I know you are probably mad at me. But we all know that hospital food is terrible. These babies have been through enough. They just need love and stability. My husband died in that hospital, a terrible place, full of sick people."

The case manager speaks up and says, "Can we see your identification? Can we please see the children? How are you related?"

The woman retrieved her identification from her purse. Tilly went to go find the children. Each girl had her own room. The rooms were clean, dainty for a girl, and loaded with toys, dolls, crayons, and coloring books.

The other officers and DCFS officers came and witnessed the rest of the home.

They interview each child and they all say they love their Mommy and are happy to stay here until Mommy comes home. Tilly takes a selfie (picture) with all of the girls. Officer Tyndall allows the girls to sit in the front of his car and play with the lights and sirens. The girls giggle with excitement, though they still appear fragile, they are happy right now.

Tilly gives the woman her card and tells her if the girls need anything please call her and she will help.

Corporal Dane drives Tilly back to her apartment and then goes back to answering calls for his shift.

Tilly piles into the couch to watch Netflix. She orders another pizza and gives strict orders for the pizza not to be commandeered by anyone but her.

The next day, Tilly goes by the house to check on the children. She brings flowers for the caregiver and candy for the girls.

An Asian woman answers the door.

"Hello. I'm Officer Tilly. I'm here to check in on the girls. May I see them please?"

"I'm so sorry but you have the wrong house ma'am."

"Isn't this 1442 Acron Street?"

"Yes, it is. But there are no children here."

Tilly stepped off the porch and looks at the outside of the house. It is the same place they had all been to yesterday. She runs back up the stairs and says,

"Look, stop playing around. I need to check up on those children."

"I am telling you, only my husband and my dog and me live here. Please come in and see."

Tilly goes into the house. Everything is the same in the kitchen, living room, and bedrooms, except there are no toys, no girls' clothing, and no crayons. There is no sign of the girls ever having been there.

Tilly calls Dane on her cellphone. "Y'all get back over here. Something is terribly wrong."

In 10 minutes, 3 units and Sergeant Hayes arrive on the scene. DCFS arrives as well. They go inside and search. There is no sign of the girls have been there.

The homeowner explains she and her husband have been out of the country; they flew to Japan for the wedding of her husband's sister. They just returned at 5 am this morning. They have airline tickets, secured parking passes, and Visas to prove it.

The case manager comes to Tilly and says, "this is the most bizarre thing. I can't explain what happened. I thought it was a miracle that they didn't have to be split up into different homes. Their Aunt Freida was so glad to take them all."

"Aunt Frieda? Janice, didn't I specifically tell you the mother did not want her children to be in the company of Aunt Frieda?"

"Yes, but after seeing how clean her house was and how good she was with them...I mean I discussed it with her and she said their mother was her sister and was mad at her because she wouldn't help her cheat people by doing their taxes illegally."

The Sergeant comes out of the house and did a BOLO (Be on the lookout) and an Amber Alert for all three young girls. He then comes over to Tilly who is sitting on the house stairs.

"Didn't you take a picture with the girls before we left yesterday?"

"I did!! I will send it to your phone." Tilly scrolls and then sends the picture.

Sergeant Hayes tells all of his squad to meet with the department's sketch artist to do a composite of Aunt Freida. He turns to Tilly and says, "I am suspending you for 3 days. Consider it a gift, since you can't seem to make yourself stay home and rest, I will help you. Here drink some water, you look like shit."

"I've never been suspended." Tilly stuttered.

"You still haven't. The next 2 days are your off days. However, the Chief and I will be at your apartment tomorrow at noon to brief you on your traffic stop. It's supposed to be hush-hush, so do not talk to anyone about it."

"Yes sir," Tilly answers, relieved that she is not in trouble.

The next morning, Tilly takes a shower and puts on jeans, a white wife-beater T-shirt, and a button-down jean shirt over. Her hair is long and she has minimal makeup on. She sprays herself with Eternity, makes herself a tall glass of iced tea, and waits for the doorbell to ring.

Exactly at 12 noon, the Chief and the Sergeant arrive at Tilley's door.

"I don't usually make house calls but you are a different kind of officer so I am accommodating your needs." The Chief said as he sat down on the sofa.

"Yes, Tilly you are a pain in my ass, but you are the best officer I have on my squad. If you repeat that I will deny it until my death." Sergeant Hayes says with a grim look on his face.

"Regarding your traffic stop, you handled it very well. We don't often work with the FBI and there are certain codes that dispatchers see when they run someone's information. The FBI was alerted and discovered you had arrested someone on their radar. They took over your prisoner and the drugs. Forgive me but these are not facts that can be disclosed openly." The Chief says.

"The guy threatened to shoot me in the head and blame the girl if I didn't stand down. They gave me made-up names when they identified themselves. For all I know it was a cartel that was taking my prisoner. Thank God I had a heat stroke or I might have had a heart attack during the process."

The Chief stands up and looks around the apartment. "Tilly, I think it's great that you are a reader and a collector. My wife collects old pottery."

He turns, looks at her, and says, "You handled the situation well. The FBI is full of some great agents. Unfortunately, you didn't get to meet the great ones. I think year after year their caseloads harden them from the inside out and they become inhuman. We are all supposed to be on the same side though it often does not appear so. The FBI has always been rouge. No new government will ever change that.

I have been advised by the Governor that we are now off the case of the missing children and the FBI will handle it from here on out."

Tilly sits down on a chair. She feels nauseated. "I promised the mother." She says quietly.

"Then that is a promise you are unable to keep. Your computer, your telephones, and all communications are to be seized by the FBI. If you even do an internet search, the FBI will be alerted. We are to stand down and deal with our local crime and adventures. Tilly, I am sure your parents told you that life is not fair."

"Yes sir."

"Okay take care of yourself and Wednesday, it's business as usual. "

Tilly nods.

The Sergeant let the Chief go out first then he put his hand on Tilly's shoulder.

"Look this FBI business is not what we do. You are great at what you do. I am proud to have you on my team. Let's help the ones we can."

"Yes sir."

THINGS ARE NOT ALWAYS AS THEY APPEAR

It Is a Saturday, the last day of the work week, at about 7 pm. Tilly receives a domestic violence call. The neighbors call saying there is a terrible fight and ask not to be involved because they are afraid.

Tilly arrives first, approaching the screen door she could see a man on top of a morbidly obese woman. He is holding a butcher knife and attempting to stab the woman. Tilly draws her gun out and begins yelling to the man, "Drop the knife! Drop the knife!" The man screams back at her, "She has the knife! I'm trying to keep her from stabbing me!" Tilly gets a little closer and realized the woman was in fact holding the knife. The man has her by the wrists trying to keep her from stabbing him. Tilly then tells the woman to let go of the knife. The woman replies, "No ma'am. I am fixing to cut this cheating motherfucker." Tilly calmly says, "Ma'am I am going to shoot you if you stab him. Please release the knife. He will still be a cheating motherfucker but you will be dead. What is it going to be?" The woman looks at Officer tilly and sees she is indeed about to shoot her. She lets go of the butcher knife and Tilly grabs it and throws it into the yard.

Tilly's partner arrives in time to help her separate the love birds. They handcuff the woman and put her in the back of Tilley's patrol car. Then they talk to the man, who is sitting on the couch. Please note this is the time that cell phones first came on the scene in America.

Tilly asks the man if he is injured. He shows about 10 small puncture wounds on his inner arms where the knife had actually cut him while he was fighting for his life. Tilly calls for an ambulance to address the injuries.

"Are there any children here?" Tilly's partner asks.

"I don't know where they at. There are 2 little bad boys around here somewhere. They saw some of this so they were probably scared." The man answers.

Tilly's partner went to go ask the woman where her kids were. She shrugs her shoulders, not caring at the moment.

Tilly asks the man to explain what happened.

"I was in the shower and she started going through my cell phone. She found a text message from my cousin, Monique, who goes by Mo, asking me to come over and fix her toilet because it is running all the time and her water bill was high. She didn't even let me explain, she just came at me with that knife. She was trying to kill me! She kept saying won't no man gone cheat on her again. I didn't cheat, I didn't do nothing."

Tilly tells the man, "Sir, your girlfriend will be charged and taken to jail. I suggest you find a new place to live. It is not safe for you to live with such a violent person. After the ambulance checks you out you need to pack your things and move out, do you understand me? Next time she may succeed in killing you."

The man sits on the couch and begins to cry. Officer Tilly says, "Sir, Do you not have anywhere to go?"

He looks at her and says, "Officer, this is my apartment. I let them move in."

Tilly's partner finds the kids hiding under a tarp in the backyard. They are terrified. He tries to comfort them but they are shaking and crying. The officer asks the oldest boy if they live here. "No sir, we live with grandma. Can you call grandma to come and pick us up?"

The officer asks, "Yes, I will. Did you guys see anything? You can tell me about anything you saw."

The smaller boy says, "Mama had a big knife and they were cussing and screaming. So, we ran and hid. It was so scary! Mama looked like a monster, her eyes were big, like bugging out and it was scary. We want to go home now can you please call Grandma?" "Do you have her telephone number?" "Yes sir, it's 741-555-1515. I had to learn it before Grandma would let us visit Mama. I sure am glad she did. Grandma is smart. Mama IS crazy!"

"Yes, she is." says the officer. "We will call Grandma to come and get you."

The boys continue to cry and hug each other, but they are relieved help has come and grandma is on the way. They are shaking and the youngest one has wet his pants.

The officer calls dispatch and gives them Grandma's number. Grandma doesn't live too far away and she is soon on the scene. She stops at Tilly's car to glare at her daughter, then she stomps into the backyard to get her grandsons.

Tilly and her partner both interview the woman who tried to kill her boyfriend. She has calmed down some. The woman admits she went thru his phone and that some whore name Mo is trying to get him to fix things at her house. "He don't even fix things here with me. How he gone fix something at Mo's house?

I bought him that phone with my income tax money and he gone talk to other girls on it? No sir that's not happening. I will kill him dead fore that happens"

The officers explain that they spoke to Monique and she genuinely is the man's cousin. His Uncle Reaves's daughter. Tilly tells the woman she will be charged with Felony Domestic Aggravated Assault and it will be up to the District Attorney if the charge is upgraded to attempted murder. The woman starts to cry and scream and rocks the parked patrol car with her tantrum.

Tilly says to the woman, "You know, I am the one who should be mad. You almost made me shoot an innocent man."

The woman begins to laugh hysterically. "I wish you had shot him. I wish you had."

Tilly explains to the woman that she cannot come back here if she happens to make bond.

"It is a law in Georgia to protect the victim. If you come back on the property, you will be arrested and held with no bond. Do you understand?"

"The woman laughed and said, "You might as well just keep me because Imma gone kill that bastard if you let me out."

Officer Tilly shared that information with the judge who raised the charges and the woman was charged with Felony, terrorist threats in addition to attempted Murder, after she felt the same way the following morning, and told the judge what she told the officer.

The Runaway husband

It is day 3 of a 4-day work week. Officer Tilly is tired and ready for a day off. She is at a red light when she gets a call from the dispatch, sending her to do a missing person report.

Tilly arrives at the address and knocks on the door. The house is pretty, with flowers in the gardens and gnomes around a fountain. It is very well maintained.

A pretty lady about 55 years old answers the door, she states she is from Korea and she married a soldier many years ago.

"For 20 years he has disappeared for weeks at a time then comes back acting as if nothing is wrong. I ask him where he has been and he ignores me until I get really upset."

Tilly asks the lady, "Why are you just reporting this now? Is something different? Has he been gone longer than a few weeks this time?"

The lady puts her hand over her own mouth as if thinking, then says, "No he has been gone for about 3 weeks but I am just worried. I have a bad feeling this time like something bad has happened."

Tilly tries to reason with the lady. "Ma'am, you have been tolerating this for 20 years. I just don't understand why now you decide to report it. Are you okay?"

"Oh yes, I am fine. His military check goes into the bank every month and I live just fine off of it. He never touches it. Officer, he is extremely weird. When he is home, he has a habit of wrapping wires around his private area when he masturbates. I don't understand it. Maybe something happened to him in the war. I don't know.

I am a good woman; I keep his house clean. But he wants nothing to do with me. My boyfriend tells me I still have good sex. So, I just don't know."

"Have you asked your husband where he disappears to?"

"I have tried to ask him where he goes and what he does. He tells me that he works for the government, he kills people and that is all he can tell me."

Tilly takes the information for the unique report, gives the lady her card, and asks her to call her when he shows up again.

Once back at headquarters at the end of the shift, Tilly uses a computer to look up the missing man's information. An address is given that is different from the one his wife resides. Tilly jots it down for the next day. She notices the man had previous arrests for attempting to hire prostitutes and harassing prostitutes.

Tilly goes home, takes a shower, and opens a beer. She is doing what she was taught not to do...reliving her day.

"Why would a man wrap a wire around his penis during masturbation? That makes absolutely no sense." She says aloud. She turns on HBO and catches up on her favorite show. She thinks is funny that HBO can't make up crap like she sees and hears every day.

The next morning, she takes a copy of her report into the Sergeant's office. He chuckles when he reads it. "Some folks, eh?"

"Yes sir. I've got a new address for the man and I am asking your permission to ask Dane and Frank to meet me over there to follow up."

The Sergeant says, "Okay but don't let them guys ask about his penis contraption." Tilly grins and then goes out to her car to begin her shift.

That afternoon Officers Dean and Frank meet her at the new address she has found. It is a nice-looking house; the lawn is clean and cut. Tilly knocks on the door as the other officers hang back. A man answers the door.

"Pardon me, sir. I am officer Tilly. I am looking for Mr. Smith. Bill Smith."

"Yes? I am Bill Smith, what can I do for you officers?" the man asks with a smile.

"Bill Smith, Date of Birth 10/05/1956?"

"Yes. The one and only."

Tilly says, "Well this is awkward sir; however, your wife has filed a missing person report on you. And I have been sent to make sure you are safe and to find out what in the name of Sam is going on?"

Bill Smith sighs and then asks the officers to please come inside his home.

All three officers reluctantly go inside. It is a beautiful home inside and out.

"I don't know where to start. When I met my wife, she was a shy but happy woman. After I married her, she became frigid, cold as a North Dakota winter. I thought she would grow out of it and warm up to me.

I thought coming to the United States was traumatic for her but that she would adjust. She never did. Forgive my frankness but sex was out of the question. So, after years of being lonely; I started looking elsewhere for comfort. My adventures eventually led me to fall in love many, many times. I am Catholic so divorce was never an option and I happen to love many different women, three of whom I settled with. I live here with them.

I have been open and honest with these three women but I could not be honest with my wife. I think I told her I was a missionary."

Tilly giggles as she corrects him, "Mercenary sir. You told her you work for the government and kill people."

"Oh yes, that is what I told her. She has always seemed agreeable to our situation. I wonder what changed?"

Tilly smiles and says, "She has a bad feeling that something is wrong and is concerned for your safety."

Tilly hesitates and then asks Mr. Smith another question. "Sir, looking over your record it appears you were arrested over 20 years ago for situations with prostitutes."

"That is correct. I wasn't always such a good judge of prostitutes, and honestly, it took a lot of hard work to find the 3 perfect women to share my life with. In my defense, I have not been arrested since being with these wonderful women."

Officer Dean pops up and says, "So let me get this right? You live here with 3 women and go home to your legal wife a week out of every couple of weeks? If all of your military retirement goes to your wife, how do you live?"

"I work. I own a machine shop in another town close to here. My common law wives work. They have already raised our children."

"Children?" all 3 officers say at the same time.

Bill Smith laughs aloud and says, "Yes, we have 6 children. All are now grown, 2 in college, 2 married, and 2 working. I have 4 grandchildren as well."

Tilly shakes her head and asks, "Sir, what am I supposed to say to your wife?"

Bill Smith looks like he is thinking, then finally says, "Tell her you found me, I am fine, and I will be home in 2 weeks. For the sanctity of my home life, I ask that you not reveal my current address or living situation. I plan to ask my wife if she will return back to Korea, to her parents. I will give her a one-way ticket there and she will still have all of my military retirement benefits."

Tilly thinks about the man's wife saying she has a boyfriend and she is not sure that she buys all of his stories but says, "Good luck to you sir. You sure know how to live on the edge."

Bill Smith chuckles and says, "Thank you." and escorts the officers out.

Once outside, Officer Dean says, "This would make a damn fine movie of the week on Hallmark Channel."

Officer Frank says, "Screw that. More like the Justice Channel when the wife kills his ass. By the way, I'm watching the obituaries from now on... I want to come to his funeral and see how this plays out!"

Tilly is just happy the other officers didn't inquire about the alleged wires around his penis.

Without Order, there is Chaos.

Rudeness is unacceptable to Pam

Dispatch: Unit 29 (Officer Tilly) be en route to the intersection of Main Street and Callaway Street. See a person about an 1850 (public disagreement).

Tilly wonders what she is facing when she sees a tow truck and a red Ford in the middle of the intersection. Traffic was backed up on both sides.

"Dispatch, this is unit 29. Could you send me someone to help with traffic?"

Tilly pulls up, turns on her blue lights, and gets out of her patrol car.

"What is the problem?" she asks. Both of the drivers start screaming at her.

"Whoa! I can only hear one at a time. Ma'am, stand over there and I will get your side in a minute. Sir, what is your name? And tell me your version of what happened."

The female begins cursing and screaming at Officer Tilly just as Officer Thomas and Officer Cornwell walk up. Tilly asks the female to please wait and that she will get her to turn to speak. The female throws her Coke bottle at Tilly, hitting her between the eyes.

Tilly is stunned but ok to finish handling the situation.

Officer Thomas immediately takes the woman into custody and puts her in his car. Officer Cornwell handles the traffic situation.

Tilly, while rubbing her head, asks the tow truck driver to please explain what is going on.

"Well, I guess her car battery went dead and she called for roadside assistance. I had a lot of other calls and it took me over an hour to get here. So, she was pissed about that. Then, her insurance said she canceled her roadside assistance months ago so it was going to be $80.00 for me to tow her car to the mechanic of her choice. She freaked out and started scratching, slapping, and punching me. I didn't make the rules, her insurance company did. Well, then she jumped in my truck, I thought she was going to try to drive away in it; then she got my keys out of the ignition, scratched the paint on the side of the truck, and threw the keys over the bridge. I have never had an experience like this before. I was terrified to touch her because I didn't want to get in trouble. Is this a nightmare?"

Tilly says, "Can you show me the scratches please?"

The man lifts the back of his T-shirt and his shirt is ripped and his back is clawed up badly, as is his neck and the left side of his face. It looked like a tiger had attacked him.

"How did she get to your back?"

The tow truck driver says, "I turned my back on her to get away and call for help and she just lunged for me. I couldn't get her off. I walked backward till she was touching the hood of my truck and I guess the heat of the hood made her turn me loose. I couldn't leave because of my keys; I called my boss to come and then she screamed she was calling the police. My boss is on the way to bring me another set of keys then we will go under the bridge to try and find my keys."

Tilly shakes her head in amazement. She looks at Officer Thomas and he drops his head to keep from smiling.

"What the hell is wrong with you Thomas?" Tilly yelled.

He pulls Tilly to a side mirror. She has a goose egg in the middle of her forehead.

Officer Thomas begins writing down all of the tow truck driver's information. Tilly walks over to Officer Thomas's patrol car to speak with the female.

The female begins kicking the window to the back door. She breaks the window as Tilly approaches. Officer Thomas runs over. They open the door, remove the female, put her in heavier restraints, a farmer may refer to it as hog tied, she is on her stomach and her feet and hands are tied behind her, rendering her unable to hurt herself or any other vehicles. They put her in Tilly's patrol car. Tilly keys up her radio, "Dispatch can you have Sergeant Stewart en route to us please?" (Sgt. Stewart was filling in for Sgt. Hayes who was out sick.)

"That's 10-4 unit 29."

The sergeant calls on another channel. "What's up?"

Tilly says, "Sir I need you to meet us here. She has kicked out Thomas' back window. Hurt my forehead, assaulted the tow truck driver. I am just not sure if she is crazy or just mean."

The other tow truck shows up and the tow truck driver's boss also arrives.

The tow truck owner says, "I really don't want this car on our lot."

Sgt confirms he is en route.

Tilley talks to tow truck owner, and said, "Sir, I understand completely, however, your business is in contract with the city of Lampton and you have to tow her car. You are under contract. To refuse would be in violation of your contract."

Sergeant Stewart arrives as Tilly is telling the Tow Truck owner what his responsibilities are.

"She is correct. Now if you want us to come to your location when or if she arrives to pick up the car, we will be happy to do that." The Sergeant says with a smile.

The tow truck owner says, "You can bet your bottom dollar on that." He then gives the stranded driver a set of keys and tells him to meet him under the bridge. The owner also tells the new tow truck driver to hitch up and get that car out of there. "Then go get checked out at the hospital."

Sergeant Stewart opens the door of Tilly's patrol car to speak to the female.

"Okay, ma'am. Now is your time to tell your version of what happened." She spits at the Sergeant and thankfully he moves quickly enough to avoid getting hit.

The Sergeant tells Officers Thomas and Cornwell to, "Transport her to the hospital to get her checked for drugs or alcohol in her system. Then transport her to the county jail once she is cleared. She is charged with 2 counts of assaulting an officer, Aggravated Assault for the tow truck driver's injuries, Destruction of public property for kicking out the window of the patrol vehicle, Theft by taking, for removing and throwing the tow truck driver's keys, Driving with an expired driver's license, and No proof of insurance. I found the driver's license in her purse. Her name is Pamela Sulley. Date of birth November 28, 1965."

Tilly offers to stay behind to clear the intersection. Sergeant Steward tells her to let Thomas take her patrol car to transport the bruiser to the hospital to get checked. Tilly laughs and says, "Okay Sergeant."

"Bring Thomas' patrol car to the shop and I will meet you there and take you to the hospital for the huge Ostrich egg you have on your forehead."

"I probably have brain damage," Tilly says with a laugh.

The Sergeant laughed and said, "Oh we already know you have that. Let's see what new damage you have from this incident"

Tilly rolls her eyes, and then laughs.

Once they arrive at the hospital they meet up with Officers Thomas and Cornwell.

The Sergeant asks. "How is our prisoner?"

Officer Thomas says, "Well, believe it or not, she didn't have any drugs or alcohol in her system when we arrived, but she is loaded up with Haldol now. She is a wild one sir! She kicked a doctor in the face and scratched 3 nurses, get this...with her toenails.".

Officer Cornwell chimes in, "I think she may be a werewolf, sir. She was howling and humping on the bed like she had a devil in her. "

Officer Thomas states, "We may need an exorcist, sir."

"Permission to call Father McDowney?" Officer Cornwell asked.

"Don't you dare! The city won't buy us any new equipment until next fiscal year, so you know they won't pay for an exorcist." The sergeant said with a laugh.

Sergeant Stewart turns to his female officer, "Come on Tilly let's get you looked at."

Tilly smiles and begins to howl softly as they walk away. The Officers crack up laughing.

The sergeant shakes his head and says, "Y'all gonna be the death of me. I am never subbing for Hayes again."

The doctor looks at Tilly and grins, "Damn girl. Do you work alone in those streets? I'm forever stitching you up for something. What happened?"

Tilly grins and says, "Back talking the Sergeant again sir."

The doctor turns to the Sergeant and says, "Dude, you have to learn to hit them where it doesn't show."

They laugh, and then Tilly tells of the prisoner throwing the Coke bottle at her.

The doctor wants to do all kinds of tests but Tilly stops him.

"Look Doc. Just give me an ice pack and a Tylenol. I am okay. If I starts feeling like something is wrong, I will come back on my own."

The Sergeant laughs and says, "Besides she's got a butt load of reports to do and court cases tomorrow."

The doctor reluctantly agrees and releases Tilly asking her to follow up with her primary care doctor as soon as possible and making her promise to put ice on her forehead.

"If it aches, or you get a headache, please come back."

She holds up 3 fingers and says, "Scouts honor doc."

The doctor shakes his head and says, "Tilly, that's the boys scout's signal. Good grief!"

Tilly goes to headquarters to finish her reports for the day, then goes home early to rest and prepare for the upcoming court cases. She puts an ice pack on her forehead and refuses to drink the Coke in her refrigerator, out of protest.

The prisoner is kept overnight at the hospital. She is restrained and there is a Deputy Sheriff from the jail who is guarding her. He steps out of the room to speak to Officer Miles and Sergeant Stewart.

"Hello, folks. Man, this is a bizarre case. She kept trying to bite me when she was awake and I think she is friends with my ex because they know the same swear words to call me."

They all chuckle. Sergeant Stewart says, "We stopped by hoping to get a statement from her. We don't even know why she acted that way or why she beat up the tow truck and its driver. Seriously, you guys use extreme caution transporting her to jail, she is definitely 1074. (Coded for mental problems)

"Rodger that sir."

Officer Miles sighs and says, "It's a shame they won't let you transport her while she is all Haldolled up."

The Deputy shrugs his shoulders and says, "I just feel bad for the correctional officers who will have to deal with her later."

The following day, Tilly and Sergeant Stewart are advised the woman is being discharged. They go to the hospital to get her statement.

Pamela Sully is still handcuffed; however, she is sitting up in the bed, smiling. She is wearing a spit guard to keep her from spitting on people.

Tilly stands by the door and the Sergeant enters. Pamela welcomes them. "Please come in. I am Pamela Sully. What can I do for you?"

The Sergeant speaks, "Miss Sully, it seems you disagreed with a tow truck and it's driver 2 days ago. Can you tell us what happened?"

"Why Sergeant, it is Sergeant?" she asks with a flirty voice.

"Yes ma'am, it's Sergeant."

"Well Sergeant, I really have only one memory of the incident. He was rude to me. I don't tolerate men being rude to me, it kind of pushes a button in my soul, and my mind goes to a distant place." Pamela purred like a kitten.

"Fair enough, Miss Sully. Have a good day." says the Sergeant, as he backs out of the room.

She calls out to Tilly, "Officer! I see you have an awful bruise on your forehead. I suggest you be careful out there on those streets. There are so mean people out there."

Tilly fights the urge to walk over and slap her.

The next day, Tilly goes to the Recorders court. She presents the charges and explains the damage. The Tow truck driver is there to testify. Pamela Sulley makes an appearance in court. She is handcuffed, has leg irons, and still has a spit guard on her face.

Judge Wilmer is a little surprised. She asks Tilly for more information.

"Your honor. I think if you let the tow truck driver explain his side it will make more sense."

"Very well, Mr.... Fox please come forward and be sworn in."

Mr. Fox did not leave out one detail of his horrible experience. His red eyes have now turned to black.

Tilly can see the look on the judge's face. This judge has compassion for the injured.

Tilly speaks up. "Your honor, I too received this injury to my face when she threw a Coca Cola bottle at me and it hit me in my forehead."

The judge shakes his head in disgust and asks," Pamela Sully do you have anything to add?" It's hard to believe this petite woman all of 4'8 and maybe 93 lbs. hurt this man this badly.

Pamela looks down casts and says, "Yeah, I'm just glad they didn't find that cocaine I had hidden in the wheel fenders. It may have been laced with something; I don't feel good at all. I feel nasty like I have been gangbanged by a bunch of cops."

The judge instructs the deputy to remove the woman from his court and take her back to the jail.

"I am going to bound this over to Superior Court. I want a complete mental evaluation of the defendant. The defendant is remanded on all charges with a one-million-dollar bond."

The public defender is stunned and offers no defense.

Tilly meets with the Tow Truck driver and tells him he will be notified when they go to Superior Court and he will need to attend and testify like he did today.

The judge clears the court except for any police officers attached to this case. The Sergeant was telling the Judge about the other officer requesting an exorcist. They have a good laugh. The Judge insists the jail put her in solitary confinement so she didn't hurt anyone.

"How could anyone so little be so mean?" the Judge asks.

"Oh, you haven't met my ex-wife I see." Officer Wirey said with a laugh.

The judge said, "I have an ex-wife. She wasn't physically mean, but mentally she could bring down a professional wrestler. For 20 years, I sat there feeling guilty about crap I never did. It was mental abuse."

"How did you get out of it?"

"One day and $20,000 worth of therapy, I had an epiphany. I'm a good guy. I deserved better. I divorced her quietly, and married my therapist...the rest is history." They all had a big laugh.

Runaway Rick

Tilly and Officer Thomas were dispatched to 1313 Argon Path about a runaway, 14-year-old,

Richard Martin. Due to his age, his last name would not be used except during the BOLO (BE ON THE LOOKOUT) His new picture and description is attached to the BOLO that all patrol officers will receive.

The officers met with the minor child's mother. They already had a picture of Richard Martin and there was already a BOLO, as Richard Martin was a habitual runaway. His parents had divorced and the minor had gone wild. His father moved out of state not leaving a forwarding address for child support reasons.

The officers felt sure, Richard's mother had made him very aware of this fact. If she did, which she denied, it was a cruel thing to tell a child. He was not a grown man; he was still a child. How awful it must feel that your own father did not want you anymore.

Each time Tilly and Officer Thomas came to the house, there was something different about Virginia Martin. New haircut, new jewelry, new clothing, new car, new furniture.

However, each time they look at Richard's room, it is the same. A bed with sheets only and a pillow with no pillowcase. The clothing that he left behind was stacked in the corner. It looked like the clean clothing was mixed with the dirty clothing. He had 2 pairs of shoes sitting on the stack of clothes. Virginia's life was increasing, while Richards's life appears to stand still.

Richard would be gone for a couple of weeks then come back for a few days, have a big argument with his mother, then take off again. Virginia would call us every time he left. She did that because Tilly told her to, in case something ever happened to Richard and she didn't report it she would be held accountable.

At Christmas Officer Thomas and some of the other male officers bought new clothes for Richard. Tilly delivered them to his house. The clothing is wrapped in brightly colored Christmas paper. Tilly explained to Virginia exactly what it is. There is also a Christmas tree that is decorated.

"I don't know why y'all bother," Virginia says, pulling on her cigarette and blowing the smoke out the back door.

"Because he is a child, Virginia. You should try too when he comes home. It is not his fault that Dan left. Dan didn't just leave you, he left Richard too. You are his family now."

Virginia doesn't answer. Tilly walks out the door.

Three days later, dispatch sends Tilly and Officer Thomas to 1313 Argon Path. As they pull up, they were surprised to see Virginia's Toyota in the drive, but Richard is standing in the road waving his hands.

"I've been home for 3 days. There is no food in the house. I'm starving. The furniture has been ripped up and turned over. There is blood in the bathroom. I had been drinking when I got home, so I cleaned up the blood and took a nap, then when I woke up, I realized I shouldn't have done that. I didn't know what to do but call you guys. I asked the neighbors to call you. Do you think something happened to Virginia?"

Tilly said, "Um Richard, she is still your mom, don't call her Virginia."

Richard looks distraught, shrugs his shoulders, and says, "I hope she is okay."

The officers told him to wait outside while they looked around. The Sergeant said to put him in the back of Thomas's patrol vehicle until he could talk to him. He only willingly got into the patrol car because the Sergeant agreed to bring him food.

Tilly and Officer Thomas secured the area until investigators arrived to see if a crime had been committed. When investigators arrived, Tilley and Thomas interviewed neighbors. The neighbor closest to Virginia's house said a black truck was there 2 nights ago, and he said he heard arguing, and what sounded like furniture breaking. He said he heard a man and a woman cursing and screaming at each other. Then after 5 minutes or so he heard the truck leave. The neighbor said he thought it was a lovers quarrel and he went to his living room to watch TV and there was no more noise. He didn't think anything else about it until Richard came knocking on his door 2 days later asking him to call the police. The police asked the neighbor to come to the station to volunteer his DNA and he declined. "I didn't have anything to do with this. I watch the movies, how y'all pin stuff like this on innocent people just to close the case. Naw I ain't giving yall nothing. I was only trying to be a good neighbor."

The officer's radio keys up and he is asked to return to the house. The detectives found Virginia's body in the basement, deceased. The boyfriend drives up, calm and confident asking for Virginia. Within 10 minutes of talking to Tilly, he breaks down and confesses. He killed Virginia because he thought she was stepping out on him.

Officer Thomas goes to get Richard some food. Tilley calls social services to come and take Richard.

About the Author

Lilly Buchanan is originally from Columbus, Georgia. She currently lives in Pascagoula, Mississippi. Lilly started writing when she was a little girl. Lilly loves pretty things, flowers, decorating, writing beautiful stories, volunteering and Jesus! Lilly has 2 amazing granddaughters, Jasmine and Alexandria. If you stop and ask she will show you pictures!!

About the Publisher

Self publishing with Draft to Digital has been an amazing experience.